11 o'Clock Chocolate Cake

Caroline Pitcher

11 o'Clock Chocolate Cake

Caroline Pitcher

EGMONT

For Patricia

Parent-type warning:
Parental/caregiver supervision recommended due
to the use of kitchen appliances.

Visit Caroline Pitcher's web site:
www.carolinepitcher.co.uk

Quotation From *Zorba the Greek* by Nikos Kazantzakis,
with kind permission from Faber & Faber Ltd.

First published in Great Britain 2002
by Egmont Books Limited
239 Kensington High Street, London, W8 6SA

ISBN 1 4052 0274 2

10 9 8 7 6 5 4 3 2 1

A CIP catalogue record for this title is available from the
British Library

Typeset by Avon DataSet Ltd, Bidford-on-Avon, Warwickshire
Printed and bound in Great Britain by Cox & Wyman,
Reading, Berkshire

This is the story of the summer just gone.

It's the story of Lizzie and Star and me,
Dodo, Pram Gran, Bottom Bob and Boss Woman,
Tuba Boy and the Beautiful Stranger.
(It's also the story of Jono Watkins and my feet.)

Who's telling this story?
Me.
Emma Peek. Known to the chosen few as M.

Life has changed for all of us this summer . . .

Don't miss the bus!

So there was Star, wandering towards the stop, when the bus came careering down the road and right through her dreams, *brrrm whoosh hiss*!

I yelled, '*Run, Star, run!*'

Everyone on the bus rubbernecked round to stare at her.

Star doesn't run if she can help it, but when she does her long legs lope great huge lopes. Her knees point to the sky. She can shift if she wants to, even at ten past eight in the morning.

She just missed being crumpled in the door as it folded shut.

'Brilliant run, Star!' brayed Someone Too Unspeakable to Think About, especially this early.

Ignore him.

'Hi, Star. Ready for E-day?' I said as she slumped on the seat in front of me.

She nodded, too puffed to speak.

Today was Tuesday, but not a normal Tuesday. Today was E-day, the start of exams, lots and lots and lots of them.

Today stretched ahead of me like a pond, all murked up with slimy weed. There was only one light which could shine through that murk like a big beacon, and that light was The Beautiful Stranger.

He was the best thing about the bus.

He was the best thing about *everything*!

great huge millipede without the hairy legs

A lot of this story happens on the bus to school, so I'd better tell you what it's like.

It's red.

It's a single decker.

It growls along the road and hisses when it stops.

It's like a great huge millipede, with wheels, of course, not hairy little legs, and only about eight wheels, not a thousand. Do millipedes have hairy legs? That's one of the Universal Questions, isn't it? Perhaps we'll never know.

> *The wheels on the bus go round and round . . .*
> *The heads on the bus go swivel and stare . . .*
> *but the people on the bus* DON'T *go chatter*
> *chatter chatter.*

Not first thing in the morning, anyway. They make sure their eyes don't meet anyone else's. They pull faces if they can't get the same seat every morning and make *grump humph*! noises. Sometimes they sit with their mouths dropped open, but they shut them before they get off. It's not a school bus, you see. It's just that a lot of us from school get on it in the mornings and in the afternoons.

The seats have blue stuff like carpets with little white and red flecky spider patterns. The seats are new and they don't smell horrible and they're not all stuck up with gum and sticky stains like *some* buses I've been on.

The driver is called Steve. He's got dark hair and an earring in the side nearest the door but I don't know if he's tall or short because I've never seen him standing up as he's always sitting down to drive our bus.

Lizzie flirts with Steve every morning. Lizzie *is* a flirt. You can either flirt or you can't.

I can't.

Steve wasn't driving that morning anyway.

packets and poems and mayo jars

By now, Star was deep in a book.

Star reads like other people breathe. She reads comics and newspapers, cereal packets, labels on mayo and marmalade jars, *The Tempest* and bus tickets. She reads poems and prattles on about Ted Hughes, Carol Ann Duffy and Benjamin Zephaniah. I've even seen her read old myths while we're *brrrm whoosh hiss*ing through the gloomy city. You know those myths, Oddy the Greek

5

goes sailing around the world, gets sung at by the Sirens and meets a one-eyed giant.

I mean, I like those stories but I wouldn't read them on a *bus*.

Star smoothed strands of hair back behind her ears. Her mum used to braid her hair and it looked great but it took hours and hours to do. When her mum went away, Star couldn't do it on her own so she just tied it back on her neck so that it fluffed out there like a feather duster.

Today she'd pulled it up and squashed it into a little knot on the top of her head, neat as the bobble on a teapot lid. All ready for exams.

I stared at that hair and wished I could do the same. I've got the wrong sort of hair. I'm not in control of my hair like Star.

I groaned, 'I don't want today! What kind of a life is this, Star?'

She turned round and said, 'Don't worry, M. It will all be fine.'

'No it won't, Star, it really won't!'

Don't get me wrong, I had done work, lots. We'd just had a week off for study leave, and before that there was half term. Takes a long time to settle, doesn't it, make sure you've got the right music and pens. I sat up in my room with my books for great huge sweeps of time, thinking how cute my writing is and admiring the lettering I had done for the headings, with different coloured pens. Pink and gold are my favourite, with curly bits and flourishes, like those old monks' illuminated books. The illuminations peaked with business studies. After that, the gold ran out.

twenty–first century illuminated business studies

So my work looked fantastic, but when I tried to see if I could remember it for exams . . .
PANIC! PANIC ATTACK!

I *had* done work. I had sacrificed suntan time. What cruel boss person put big exams in the summer? Just look at my legs! They were golden-brown on the front and ice-cream white on the back. I needed to tan, not revise.

Oh well, I told myself, after exams I can make up for lost tanning time. We'll have lots of time off, and then it's the summer holidays, if the sun hasn't blown up or fizzled out by then.

'I can't wait for the exams to be over,' I said. 'I'm longing for doss–around time.'

Star was staring through the window. She didn't answer me.

A voice inside my head said, Star has been different lately. I couldn't say how. I mean, Star is often far away from us in her own little solar system. She likes it up there. But today she had a feeling wrapped all around her, like an atmosphere.

Whoops! The bus stopped with a hiss of brakes and everyone toppled to the end like Pringles down the packet.

Stand-in-Steve

Lizzie's stop. I saw her scowling because as I now realised it wasn't Steve the Bus. (I don't notice Steve the Bus really because I don't fancy him.)

Maybe the driver who wasn't Steve the Bus but was Stand-in-Steve hadn't known about this stop until he'd almost driven into it?

Lizzie sat down next to me. Lizzie is about the only person I can cope with first thing in the morning (except for Basil). Star and I are good friends but Star is shy, even with Lizzie and me, and we both need our space first thing. An ice rink might do.

Lizzie put on her Truly Tragic face. She wailed, 'What a start to the day! No Steve.'

'It's hot, Lizzie! Maybe he's taken the day off and gone to Skegness.'

'I bet he's at the Lido,' she said. 'Mmm . . . ready to dive into the pool in very small trunks . . . think of him, M.'

I did. Skinny legs and wibbly-wobbly bits. Waist like the middle of an accordion . . . like my dad . . .

So I said, 'He's a bit old.'

She ignored that. She said, 'How much did you do, M?'

'How much what?'

'Science, of course,' she said. 'I worked all night. But now there's nothing in my brain at all. I've put too much in there and the lid won't shut and it's all fallen out again. Oh M! *Look* at your nails! Dodo will do his pieces when he sees them!'

fingernail interlude

'Dodo won't even notice,' I said. 'He'll be too busy sighing. Anyway, doing my nails calms me down. It's like meditation.'

I held up my hands for a better view. Each nail was a different colour, deep purple, black, blue, bronze, gold, pearl, hot pink, emerald and silver (twice. My fave.).

'Blimey, M!' growled The Unspeakable One from Way back Down. 'Have you got a licence for those nails? I'm glad I've got my sunglasses on.'

Scathe . . .

I didn't bother to turn round.

Jono Watkins always has some comment to make about me. It's never nice. He thinks he is superior and funny. He's got two big brothers to imitate. Maybe they have S&S. Style and Sophistication.

He hasn't.

I didn't even TUT. Lack of TUT would show him he was quite beneath contempt.

'I suppose your toenails are equally impressive.' He never gives up, doesn't Jono Watkins.

'You suppose wrong!' I said. 'And you can blame Basil for that.'

(That is a Basil Bad Thing. He stops me varnishing my toe nails. The other is his breath, because Basil is a garlic thief.)

'I mean, what is the point of decorating your toes, M, babe? No one can see them.'

Shut up about my feet, Jono Watkins, shut up!

You see, I have a secret. A shameful secret . . .

Just in time we *brrrm whoosh hiss*ed up to

the Most Important Bus Stop that is at the Very Centre of the Universe

My eyes searched for their favourite fill-in, their perfect panorama, and it was *Hot Breath, Hammering Heart!*

People were slumped around the bus stop as if they might faint in the sunshine.

There were lots of faces, but only one came into focus, the one I had been waiting to see.

The Beautiful Stranger!

He wasn't there *every* morning. I had been keeping a diary entitled *The Daily Sightings of my Stranger*. Nothing more, in case Jono Watkins ever found it when he noses around. I wrote *The Daily Sightings* every morning in registration. Dodo (more soon) thought I was working. He was always pleased to see me quiet and 'occupied' as he called it. (Sounds like a bog.)

Unfortunately, I could find no pattern to the Beautiful Stranger being at the Mst. Imp. Bus Stop at the V. Cntr. of the Uni.

Which bus does he wait for . . . and when, and how often . . .? Please let him get on our bus one morning . . . but what would I do if he did?

He was *so* good-looking. His hair flopped gleamily onto

a suntanned brow, all variegated, the hair I mean, some dark and some blonde, a bit like Basil's tail, although Basil's tail was born like that, he is not a dyed dog. What you see is what you get in Basil's case.

The Stranger's eyes looked deep and dark as caverns, although if I'm honest it was hard to tell from the bus. He was so cool, as if he didn't care what was all around him.

I'm sure he was somewhere else in his mind. He was nonchalant. That's a good word, I thought, that's just how he is. I said it softly to myself, over and over again like a mantra, 'Nonchalant nonchalant nonchalant . . . OM.'

That morning he must have felt me looking at him. He didn't look away. He looked right back, deep into my soul. I wanted to melt (like dark chocolate over a pan of boiling water when you're making Eleven o'Clock Chocolate Cake. More later).

The stare lasted ages because it was Tuba Time.

Tuba Time

Tuba Time is on Tuesdays. We'd be at the Mst. Imp. Stop for hours, which was fine by me, because of the Beautiful Stranger, but, you see, small Year Seven plus great huge tuba equals long long wait for him to clamber onto the bus. Fancy giving someone so little such a great huge instrument! I'm a flute woman myself.

He came staggering up the steps with it, bashing it against the sides. His face flushed red as sweet-and-sour sauce. You know, the kind of sauce you put on Late Night Noodles?

Late Night Noodles is? are? a truly multi-ethnic dish for the twenty-first century. Make this amazing dish Your Very Self! Get your parent to acquire these simple ingredients. Get a pan of boiling water. The water isn't multi-ethnic, it's probably from the River Trent with a squirt of bleach to kill all the diseasy things wriggling around on it and poison you with bleach instead.

LATE NIGHT NOODLES*

excellent for your sleepover. However, it's all ever so red so your parents will moan about the washing-up. And don't leave your noodles on their own while you go off and paint your nails or they will burn out the bottom of the pan.

You will need:
- **lots of packets of traditional nest noodles (from Thailand or Manchester)**
- **one pot of Szechuan sweet–and–sour sauce (from some superior supermarket or other)**
- **water**

1. boil noodles in water
2. pull them apart
3. slosh on pot of red sauce

Eat with chopsticks if you want to be a poser, fingers if you are hungry.

WING YIP!

Noodle interlude over.

Everyone watched the red–faced Year Seven battling with his tuba. Watching made him worse. He tried hard not to bash. The harder he tried, the more he bashed.

Today he bashed Boss Woman.

'Sorry!' he mumbled.

'It's all right,' she said. 'You just got my briefcase.'

It was a smart shiny briefcase, but she's a smart shiny woman. I bet she keeps a spare pair of her smart shiny tights in there, just in case she snags the ones she's wearing. That's what the magazines say you should do, and I bet Boss Woman's spare tights are in that briefcase under her sandwiches which are not your common cheddar cheese and pickle, more like roasted vegetables, sun dried prawn, and langoustine tikka. Or maybe she goes out for lunch with her shiny friends and picks at feng shui sushi and mineral water with a hint of mango.

background notes on Boss Woman

Boss Woman has lots of Style and Sophistication, unlike Jono Watkins who only thinks he has. She was on our bus every morning, skin so clear and so tanned, blouse so white, skirts so short and straight, jackets so sleek and tailored except when it was hot. Not that Boss Woman would sweat, not that she'd ever have great huge ponds under her pits like Mr Pimm in Chemistry.

She had glacé cherry lips and one of those haircuts that

scream *money*! – you know, all scissored and razored and tapered into her neck. She had little highlighted bits, ash blond and silver. She was so streamlined, cool but corporate, never floaty old tat or naff ethnic-spend-no-time-on-it like my mum.

How old was Boss Woman? Not as old as my mum, but then, very few women are.

Boss Woman was too smart to be anyone's mum, so who could she boss around at home? I bet she bossed loads of people at work. Lizzie and I had decided she was Head Exec Chick of Tesco or the Liberal Democrats, maybe even Next.

But then why did she go on the bus? She didn't look as if she was an eco-warrior into green public transport, not in *those* tights.

The Ring Fairy had visited Boss Woman some months ago. I noticed before Lizzie did. It was hard not to notice because Boss Woman kept waving her hand around, holding on to rails when the bus went round corners. *Mmmmm* . . . very nice.

The ring on her third finger twinkled in the sunlight. It hung there like a ten-tonne weight, a great huge mountain of big blue flashers with foothills of dazzling white. Lizzie said the foothills were diamonds, of the Koh-I-Noor quality. Any more jewels and her finger would bend double.

This morning Boss Woman looked at the flashers and dazzlers and sighed deepest sorrowful. Some people are never satisfied with their lot, are they?

more dosh, less spinach!

Tuba Boy was even deeper Szechuan red by now. He was so flustered, he didn't know where to go, but Star patted the seat next to her. She smiled at him. Relief shone on his little red face and he flopped down *phoomph*!

I thought, *that's* more like Normal Star. She is kind to little kids. Her dad got a new woman last year, Partner as he calls it – her, and so Star has ended up with a step-brother and step-sister, although I've hardly ever seen them. Once Lizzie and I called round for Star and they just stared round the door at us.

I wish my sisters stayed behind the door. Lucky Star – *she* hasn't got pesky little siblings. I have two. It's worse if children have Something To Do With You, and mine are blood relations all right – they make me feel like spilling blood at least once a day. This morning there was a row of teeth – along the bathroom windowsill. It looked as if someone had been digging for bits of dinosaur. The rooty parts were still blood-red. My sister Sophie had lost a lot of teeth over the last couple of weeks, ever since the Tooth Fairy started to leave a pound a visit. I think Sophie yanked them out because she was saving up for a new game to go in her collection along with *Wrench, Crossbow Creepies, Truck Madness, Doom Devils* and *I'll be back, you suckers*!

So unfair. I used to get twenty scabby pence a tooth, less than anyone else in my class! *My* Tooth Fairy had never heard of inflation. Because I'm the eldest of three my parents go, 'Emma, darling firstborn, we tried things out on you. We can relax a bit more with the others, now we know we've got you right.' They smile their smug parent smile at each other.

What they mean is, 'We held you in our sights like great huge cats with a mouse' (or foxes with a dear little fluffy bunny is a better mettathing). 'You turned out all right, no mass murders, eating disorders (except for chocolate addiction) no heroin takings or multiple pregnancies at twelve, so we can be soft on your sisters.'

But the damage is done. My name is Emma Peek and I am a chocoholic.

I suffered, *oh how I suffered*, for the sake of parental enlightenment. Strict baby bedtimes, sweets once a year and no public chewing gum, music lessons every week whatever else I wanted to do, wholewheat home-made pizza, all crumbly muck brown, with bits of vegetable on top, vegetable that *had once lived in the real brown earth and was not ashamed*!

I was fed cakes with not a lot of sugar, fresh fruit salad (for a treat! ha! ha! ha!) when friends came round, fruit salads with *live fruit*! *The embarrassment was too great huge.*

I suffered unspeakable spinach.

If they'd ever bothered to consult me I'd have said, 'A tenner a tooth, please. *More dosh, less spinach.*'

great huge yawn

The Stand-in-Steve fumbled about with something and the bus lurched away.

Now that I'd seen *The Beautiful Stranger* the rest of the day gaped like a great huge yawn.

'The last thing I ever want is an exam,' moaned Lizzie, rolling big eyes.

Let me tell you about Lizzie. She is a drama princess. She can sing and dance and act and really shovel it on and make grown parents and heartless teachers weep during school plays.

Tell her to be Ophelia with PMT, Bette Davis coughing on a fag, Little Nell all pathetic 'n' dying, Lady Macbeth all wailing and scrubbing blood off her hands, and at once she *is*.

She doesn't act a part. She's taken over. Her eyes can fill with soul and sorrow. They can flash. They can melt concrete and drive boys bonkers.

Now she sighed with everything she'd got, and scrabbled in her bag for a science book. It looked as if someone had cleaned the bath with it. She flicked through the pages far too fast to read anything, like shuffling a pack of cards. I thought it was a bit late to revise but I didn't like to say so. The Year Seven had plonked his big long tuba case across the aisle so everyone would have to step over it. He'd stretched out his legs and was resting his feet on it. He sat chomping his pencil, a book open on his knees. I peeped over the seat and saw scabby pencil scrawl. He must have been catching up on his homework. Too much tuba playing last night, I suppose, because in my experience you get your homework done straight away in Year Seven. You're innocent, you're eager, you're pure and untainted. When you've spent years in secondary school, as I have, it's a different story. It's hard, it's ever so hard being sixteen, really truly and ultimately.

'M! I almost forgot!' cried Lizzie. 'We're online now. I'm going to e-mail you tonight. You can e-mail me, M!'

'E-mail? Or *Ee! Male!*'

My Yorkshire dialect was lost on Lizzie. She pulled a face. Lizzie is slow to get my jokes.

'Hang on, let me write it down,' I said, grabbing her science book. 'See? Geddit?'

'Uh-huh! Very funny, M.'

'Now give me your address.'

'I'm – ooh, I'm not sure – er – Lizzieluscious@bigfoot-polka-dots-and-lots-more-dots or something. I think. What's yours?'

'I can give you mine when I e-mail you, Lizzie.'

'But I might e-mail you first. C'mon, M.'

'Right. I'm M@madhouse.co.uk.'

Lizzie wrote it in her science book.

The Year Seven was now scribbling furiously. Then he only put his pen in his mouth and spluttered so that his lips went all blue. Could have been worse. Could have been asphyxiation. You know, computers are safer than pens. The internet has no lids to choke on.

Service withdrawn

Let me explain here – I am a net princess. As well as nagging me to get off the phone, even though I save them hundreds of pounds by using my mobile, the parents nag me to get off the internet. Of course I'm usually there because I am doing homework. The parents threaten to pull the plug on the internet. The parents say the service may be withdrawn.

Lizzie wants to become a net princess too but she needs practice. She is not patient. I'm not sure it's her true medium.

Star as a net girl? Star is technophobic. She needs paper pages, then she can cope. Bits of her brain seem to have service withdrawn.

Lizzie said, 'I hope there's enough room on the net for all your prattle, M.'

You see, some people think I talk a lot.

I will be silent for a while and worry her.

I gazed at the back of Star's neat head.

Strands of gold gleamed against the dark.

what I am like really (really?)

My hair has never gleamed gold or black. It's bunny-coloured. I've seen country bunnies on picnics. I mean our family's picnics, not the bunnies' picnics. My hair is the same colour as their fur. Dull.

There's a village in Scotland called Dull. We passed the signs for it on holiday. Bet it was more fun than our car, with my little sisters screaming and squabbling and my father groaning, 'How can you want to go *again*! Four females, and one of them always wants a toilet,' and my mother grumbling about coffee and three pregnancies.

My hair is dull. I've tried adding interest with a tube of Cherry Brown but my hair went brassy orange, like Widow Twanky from the pantomime I had to go to last Christmas because I've got little sisters.

It was quite funny, actually.

Then I tried Autumn Gold but it made my hair go Autumn Purple, the colour of blackberries when they squash in your hand when you're picking them for your mother to make blackberry and apple crumble which she hardly ever does because she witters on about her weight so you get extra and she watches every mouthful you eat, just like Basil does.

After Autumn Gold I gave my hair a rest. It went back

to dull bunny but at least it didn't feel like a pan scourer. Even without dye, my hair goes all wild and woolly unless I spend hours doing it and smothering it in mousse/gel/defrizzer/yukky thickening serum or straightening balm, whatever the shops can offer that Saturday.

I'm sort of middle height, and not really fat or thin.

I don't know what I look like really. You can't look at yourself like you look at a stranger, can you? And in photographs I always look silly, all posed and artificial. I hardly recognise myself.

'Is that me?' I ask. 'Is that I?'

I am quite pale but not pretty china-white. More uncooked pastry. My parents are both quite fat and extra-white. Parental sad factor? Higher than average.

Lizzie has one quite white mother and one plywood-coloured father. He's from Greece. Why did he come to this damp land? Lizzie calls him George the Patriarch, but it's her mum who runs everything. They all shout a lot in Lizzie's house.

Lizzie has dark skin and amazing thick black hair. Sometimes she puts a bit of henna on so there are shines of mahogany and crimson.

Star's mother has been away teaching in France this year, so she has only got her dad around. Star says his new partner is like him this time, biological white and Midlands. Star is what JoJo and Carly at school call 'light-skinned'. (JoJo and Carly are definitely black.) When Star has to fill in stupid forms I suppose she has to put a tick in the 'mixed' box which is a bit silly because all races are mixed up, especially the British. We spend years and years of school yawning over Vikings and Romans and Normans and Celts and things taking us over and then baldies in Union Jack T-shirts screech on about racial purity and curry. You see them in town on Saturday afternoons.

Star's mum's granddad was West Indian from Trinidad. Jono Watkins said he must have been a Trini-Granddad. (Ho ho ho, Jono Watkins.) Anyway, Star once explained that the Trini-Granddad married a Malaysian mum, but really they came from Erdington which is in Birmingham, and then their daughter, Star's mum, married her dad who came from Nottingham.

So this all just goes to show that Star is not boring-looking like me. She says she wants to go to Trinidad and Malaysia but neither the Trini-Granddad nor the Malayan-Grandmum want to go and check out their roots as they're supposed to do. They never leave Erdington. Star goes to see them when her mum comes over for a few days.

I've got boring beginnings. Maybe I will be reborn as a bunny? My nose has got a whiffly bit at the end. Someone once said that it wiggled when I talk. I think a bunny's life might be hard work, having loads of babies while waiting to be shot by a grumpy old farmer.

the Boob Fairy/Knocker Sprite

She is the Bad Fairy at the feast in my opinion.

The Boob Fairy visited me early with two quite big huge breast dollops. I'm not really at one with them yet — or at two. Lizzie is happily at ease with hers. They stick upwards and outwards, they are truly noticeable, and men do notice them. Lizzie doesn't mind, in fact she's always sticking them out.

I do mind my dollops being noticed. I would like to do a sort of binding, like the Chinese used to do, only on dollops, not feet, so the dollops don't wobble and call attention to themselves. Star is minute in the breast department.

the Foot Fairy

A kind one, the Foot Fairy.

Mind you, I offer at her altar — I put *hours* of work into my feet. And I had plans for them; I'd seen a woman on telly doing great nails, with little transfer seahorses, pigs and mobile phones, Ferraris too. Must get some for my feet. I did file my toenails to points but it wasn't good on tights. I might do that again in the summer holidays and look into henna tattoos, and toe-rings. (Not toe-piercing. I am into good looks, not pain.)

When I am rich I shall employ a nail technician, a hair stylist and a hunky personal trainer.

On this terrible exam morning, you couldn't see my

feet. They were locked up in my school shoes. But they really *feeture* (geddit?) at weekends when my toes are revealed to the world. Even worse than naked nails are tatty ones. Supposing I had an accident and ended up in hospital! It would be almost as bad as wearing old knickers.

When I'm in sandals, or barefoot, people compliment me on my feet. I like my feet. I can see them easily. They're kind of separate from me. The rest is all stuck together in a great huge lump.

My feet are special.

They are my very best thing.

It wasn't always so. Jono Watkins could tell you all about that.

But it's a shameful, *shameful* secret. I will kill him if he ever gives it away.

more details

What else do you need to know? I talk quite a lot . . . I think I may be a bit noisy sometimes. Dodo Dollop says I'm FAR TOO LOUD.

He goes, 'Emma Peek! Emma Peek! Emma Peek!'

That's his 'joke' because he says I make enough noise for three.

Noisy? *Moi*? Well, maybe I am, but I'm noisy because life is exciting, unless you're Dodo Dollop, of course.

Live, Dodo, why don't you?

what Dodo Dollop is like

He's not really Dodo Dollop. He's Mr Donaldson, so we called him Donald and that became Dodo because of he has a big beaky nose and a flumpy walk but he isn't extinct and then Adam who is one of the Wot Kin, (the Unspeakable Jono Watkins' henchmen) wanted to call him plain Dollop, but I fought against that because it made me think of breast dollops although I didn't tell Adam that of course, and so we compromised and called him Dodo Dollop. It's all obvious, really.

He sighs all the time. He is Mr Donaldson, form tutor, maths teacher, wearer of terrible jumpers and great huge ears which stick out.

Lizzie and I decided long ago that his sad factor is right off the scale. We have wondered whether to suggest Blu-Tak for the ear problem? Some kind of restraint or ear brace, maybe.

My mother says Dodo is quite attractive, but then what does *she* know?

He wears two-in-one trousers. You know, those ones with the zip-off legs. He can zip off his legs and cycle home in shorts, reinforced seat and all.

He hums. I mean, he hums tunes, not that he smells. He seems to be able to keep himself clean, so that's a plus. So are his Zebra Mints. Dodo buys vast bags of stripey mints for us. He calls them Zebra Mints but I don't know what they're called in the shop. He hands them round at break most mornings, and especially at exam time. They are so chewy and minty. You should hear those papers rustle.

He loves music, does Dodo Dollop. He calls it music anyway. Most of it is truly terrible. We bring music to play on the last day of term. He always gets in first with a load of old Beethoven, or the Eels, and takes over the CD player with his dreary Dodo stuff.

Last Christmas it was Bach, JS and then a man called Santana. I thought at first Dodo was talking about Father Christmas. No. This Santana man looked like a tramp in a Tyrolean hat and played waily guitar for old folks' salsa dancing they do when they imagine they are hip.

I've told Dodo, I've said, 'Why can't you play real music like a real person, sir? It'll be Jimi Hendrix if you're not careful, and then you'll be a real true saddo!'

Dodo stared at me, all disbelief. His voice went all low and he said, 'Hendrix made celestial music, Emma.'

He wasn't joking. I know he wasn't. I had touched a nerve all right.

Then he said, 'Volume control stuck again? You could always get a job as a foghorn, Emma!'

How could he mention that three-letter J word?

You see I don't know what to *do* when I leave school.

I have no idea about jobs. Everyone keeps saying, 'And what are you going to do, Emma?'

I don't know! *PANIC*! *PANIC ATTACK*!

Dodo *may* have a point about my volume control. I'm not quiet like Star. She's keeping it all in. In fact, that way

I think she is a bit odd. I mean, she's not like many other people I know.

She's quiet, she's secret but it's all going on inside her head, you can tell. And what is going on inside Star's head is completely different to what is going on inside other people's. She makes me think of a pearl inside an oyster shell. There! That's almost poetic enough for Star herself. She doesn't try to be cool or keep up, and I like that, I don't like everyone trying to be the same. The bus stopped outside school. We don't need to ring the bell. Steve, real or Stand-in, stops anyway. Shame. But at least I could write up *The Daily Sightings* while Dodo tried to organise everybody.

I think that now we need to draw a veil across these E-days at school, for they are truly terrible. BUT, soon I can tick off an exam on my exam timetable. It took me ages to design in gold and pink and purple. It is a drawing of a real table with clocks in each corner and a bendy trail of subjects, a bit like a bus route, but not in order, cos I thought it might be a surprise to me which ones I have done and can cross out and which ones are left. All right, so it isn't. I'll know next time. There is maths Spanish art English language English literature music history science ICT and a little bit of textiles.

AAGH!

When I got home that night I *only* had to go straight out again!

Where?

Bob's.

There are two shops near us, one on top of another, and they're both Bob's. Both shops boom with country and western music which is truly terrible.

Bottom Bob's is the downstairs. It sells veg and frozen food, baked beans and fizzy drinks, parents' wine and Bacardi and sweets.

Top Bob's is the upstairs. The stairs wind up from just by the biscuits. A big green finger on the wall points to

Cards Gifts and
Many Kwality Fancy Goods.

At the top of the narrow windy stairs, Bob sells everything else there is, tights and slipper socks with teddies on them, great huge knickers with yards and yards of elastic, string and cards, toys and plastic gladioli, china ladies with shepherd's crooks and crinkly bits, and alarm clocks with pink and smiley faces. Anything you can't eat, really, unless you're Basil, who can chew anything.

That night my mother made me go to Bob's for cucumber. I mean, why can't she shop properly?

To pamper myself I bought sweets too, flying saucers and blackcurrant bootlaces. It's my Inner Child, you see, who was deprived of sweets all those years.

I finally managed to turf my dad off the computer at about eight o'clock. He went off, muttering about his accounts and invoices, but *I* know he'd spent an hour with Lara Croft.

Go away, Dad.

I had a new message! I thought, Lizzie has beaten me to it.

I clicked on 'get new message'.

Guess what it was! You can't! It was –

> *We haven't met. Yet. Hope we will meet soon!*
> *I C U on the bus most mornings.*
> *Have U got Xams soon? U read books a lot.*
> *Keep cool.*
> *Craig*

WHAT?

I had to read and re-read it five hundred times. My heart shot up inside me like a lift!

It was HIM! It had to be, didn't it! Did I reply? Should I? Shouldn't I?

Should I reply straight away, or leave it to look as if I'm cool and in demand, out all the time . . . I wrote back straight away.

> *dear Craig*
> *I C U 2 Yes I've got Xams but a swot I am not.*
> *Maybe we can meet at the weekend.*

M. (That's what my friends call me. My other name is Emma).

What did I have to do next? I had to play my flute. I always do that when things are really good and I can't settle! I put on lots of eye make-up and wild up my hair even more than it is. I catch sight of myself in the mirror and think, I am a nymph with floaty hair. I imagine myself in a girls' band. Basil likes to listen to me play, turning his head from side to side.

I couldn't sleep. I didn't try. I didn't want to, cos if I was asleep I couldn't gloat to myself about the e-mail and The Beautiful Stranger whose name is Craig. What a wonderful name! I've always liked the name Craig.

I thought, I'd like to put blond Craig on a cake stand and turn him round slowly, look at his hair and dark brown eyes and broad back and lovely bottom (although you can't see that much when he's standing at the bus stop looking for buses.) Every time I thought about that nonchalant blond cool handsome languid laddo, and his highly accomplished e-mail, I felt I could jump right over that moon in the sky, shouting *WING YIP!* as I went!

When I thought of Craig, (every second of every minute) I thought of toffee. Guess it was the colour of his eyes, mixed with his sweet gorgeousness . . .

I must have fallen asleep THUD because I woke up with Mum nagging, 'You'll be late, Emma! You'll miss the bus! Then I'll have to drive you to school! Then I'll be late for my class!'

Don't they go on about nothing at all! My mother teaches pottery to adults who should know better. There are ordinary adults and old ones and others who missed out on education hundreds of years ago or find it really hard. She says some of them use it for therapy. My mother, in charge of therapy? Ha! She has classes three mornings a week starting at half past nine, and boy do we know about it.

She needn't have worried. The last thing I wanted to do was miss that bus.

I mean, I wouldn't mind missing school but I did want to sit on that bus and see Craig.

if Jono Watkins was a car . . .

'Stand-in-Steve *again*!' moaned Lizzie as she settled her bottom on the seat. 'And he doesn't know what's happened to Real Steve. I am a desperate woman. But hey, come on, M, we'd better talk e-mail.'

What? *How did she know already*?

'What *about* what e-mail, Lizzie?' I said. I'd make the suspense last as long as I possibly could.

'Well, you didn't get a message from me, did you?'

'Oh . . . no. I suppose I didn't, Lizzie.'

She turned and frowned at me.

'Nice of you to notice, M,' she huffed. 'I thought you'd

be cross you didn't get one. There's some problem with the servant or something. We have to sort it. We –'

I couldn't wait for her to stop waffling about the server doofers, I wanted to tell her what was really important, like, 'I *did* get an e-mail from Someone Else!'

Come on, Lizzie, ask me who . . .

'Who?' asked Lizzie.

I didn't answer straight away because I was keeping watch, but HE wasn't at his stop today. Disappointment swamped me like a wet tent at Brownie camp.

'How am I going to last till tomorrow?' I wailed. 'I don't even know I'll see him then. He's not there every morning. He's unpredictable.'

'Oh dear me! No Noddy Nonchalant! Trage-deee,' growled a voice from the seat behind me. Jono Watkins must have heard my mantra yesterday. *How hard* was he listening with his great huge nosy flapping ears?! I *HATE* him. I'm not giving you Background Notes on him, because then he might think he is important. Let me just tell you that in Year Seven a writer woman came to talk to us. She was utterly mad with enormous earrings. She taught us a kind of writing game, called IF . . . And I'm telling you, IF Jono Watkins was a mammal he'd be a great huge grinning orang-utan. IF he was a flower he would be a smelly old fly-eating sundew. A jewel? Imitation. Musical instrument? Flugelhorn. Bird? A Blue-footed Booby.

I asked him once what kind of car he thought he

was. 'A red Ferrari, of course, M babe!' he cried.

'No, Jono. A Robin Reliant. In beige,' I said.

Then Star cried, 'Uh-Oh! There goes Pram Gran!'

Pram Gran

We saw Pram Gran a couple of times a week.

Today she was wearing her pink hairnet. She was always in such a hurry, rushing along, bent over, pushing her pram. It wasn't a buggy, it was one of those big springy old-fashioned prams.

And in the pram? Her grandchild, you're thinking? Sweet little babby in a crocheted bonnet?

That's what we thought the first time we saw her, but one Saturday we passed her in the street and had a real good peer.

It was a dog.

It was tucked up in blankets with its head on a flowery pillow.

'She must love that dog so,' said Star. 'She's very old to rush around like that.'

Lizzie said, 'Yes, but at least she's keeping her hair tidy. Now, M, don't try my patience any more. Who's this e-mail from? Remember who you are and don't try to be so mysterious!'

I tried to be mysterious for a hundredth of a second, but I can't keep things to myself so I said, 'The Beautiful Stranger at the bus stop e-mailed me last night and he said have I got exams and he'd like to meet me and his name is Craig.'

'Must be mad, sad, deaf and blind,' muttered Somebody Unspeakable.

I shouted, 'I can't hear you, Jono Watkins! Get out of my life and back in your box!'

'Where will you meet him?' asked Lizzie.

That was a tricky one. I could see parent problems if he wasn't some safe nerd from school that somebody else's parents knew, had been watched by the whole parent club for every single second of his life at playgroup, nursery, blah blahty blah, he could read the *Guardian* and count to a thousand and ten when he was three months old. Parental interference is a serious problem. Mum would probably suggest I took my dear little sisters along with me to meet him. She's always doing that. I might have to involve my friends . . .

'I hope that's not all she has,' said Star, still thinking Pram Gran. 'I hope it's not a love substitute. Do you think she is a lonely soul in mourning?'

'No. I just think she's cracked,' said Lizzie.

I don't think Lizzie was ever headed for a career with the elderly or unwell . . .

Suddenly Star turned to me and smiled. 'M, I should have said! I'm really pleased for you. I could tell by your face the moment I got on the bus something good had happened. You're all pink and your eyes are shining.'

'Thanks.'

I thought, Star's feeling better today. Fancy her noticing all that about me!

Star isn't her real name. One of the reasons she's called that is because she will get starred A's in her exams. Maybe that's why she's so with it this morning? Maybe it's the thought of more exams to star in?

No. She's not like that. She never boasts or shows off her grades. She just takes it all as a matter of fact. I think she really likes work. Exams are just an extra treat in her day.

the Basil Project

When I got home I shut myself away in my room. I just wanted to think about Craig.

Fat chance.

'Emma! EMMA? What are you doing?'

'Revising. I've got exams, remember? And I *don't* want to go to Bob's, Top or Bottom, especially if it's for spinach!'

'Oh. I wondered if you'd give Sarah a hand with some writing. She's got to read a project in assembly tomorrow. And Sophie keeps annoying her.'

Well *there's* a surprise. My little sisters fight, and I mean *fight*, nails and teeth sometimes (if Sophie hasn't already pulled all hers out for the Tooth Fairy). They fight wherever they are. In the car, in the bathroom, and *espesh* in the supermarket.

'Oh Mum! Can't you do it?'

'I've got to cook tea, Emma!'

Sophie could do it. She could help her sibling. She never did. She's always taking up valuable computer space, playing one of her horrible fantasy games (maniac at the wheel of a fast car, or hero lost in the labyrinth with monsters lurking in broom-cupboards).

Oh well . . . Sarah had paper placed straight in front of her on the kitchen table, pencil sharpened to a fine and deadly point. She meant business.

I suppose I had better get in the parental good books if I am ever to get out on my own with Craig.

'Emma! This is the Basil Project!' announced Sarah. 'First of all, what sort is Basil?'

'He's a silly,' I said.

'No! Is he – he's not a spangle, is he? Or a peekaboo?'

'No, Sarah. He's not any sort.'

'But Mrs Collins wants to *know*.'

I sighed. I looked down.

Basil looked back up at me. He made that little snorting noise he does and then *vroom*! Straight on to my knee. His legs were short, but full of spring. They could jump, believe me.

'What *sort*, Emma?' screeched Sarah.

I looked at Basil's long nose, button-black eyes and enormous tatty ears. He yawned with a squeak. His pink tongue stretched towards me like a chameleon's and the updraught from his tail sent Sarah's paper floating off the table.

Basil didn't look real. He could have been one of

those Wombles that were on telly ages ago. He's sweet. Sweet but smelly. One of the reasons for his smelliness is his passion for garlic. My parents buy big bulbs of garlic to cook their weird stuff. Basil sniffs out that garlic with his long nose. He loves to carry it. It's just Basil size. It's his trophy, it's his prize. He scuttles off with the whole bulb of it and hides it in his bed, then chomps away at it when my mother has forgotten to buy him a bone or a chew.

'Basil isn't a sort, Sarah,' I explained. 'He has no sort. We don't know about his mum and dad because he's from the dogs' home. The vet said he's got a bit of Doberman and lots of Dachshund, some Setter and Rottweiler. But he ended up small. He's a real mixture.'

Sarah picked up her pencil. 'How do you spell Basil?' she said.

I printed the word in her spelling book. I know what to do. I often get collared for homework. It should be the parents' responsibility! They neglect their duty, say they have to cook and work and wash, and other feeble excuses.

Sarah stuck out the tip of her tongue towards her nose and began to write.

The pencil point snapped so we had to sharpen up again.

She wrote, 'The sort of dog Basil is is a Reel Mixcha.'

'Good job we've been doing *ch* words,' she said. 'Why is he called Basil?'

'Why not?' I said. Then I thought, better explain.

'When we got him I wanted to call him Tramp cos he was wandering the streets. Mum said Tramp was not a nice name and not politically correct and he looked just like Basil Brush who was a scabby fox who was on telly when the parents were alive. OK Sarah?'

'OK Emma.' She frowned. She didn't write anything down about Why Basil Is Called Basil.

We spent a long time on Basil work – fave food, fave walks, foot size – and let me tell you here Basil is the only dog I've met whose feet really smell. It's as if he had worn two pairs of little old trainers.

Uh-oh, we're on dangerous ground . . .

Sarah began to draw him.

Mona Basil

Basil is very drawable and paintable. I often pencil-draw him or charcoal him and I've done him in water-colour and pastel *but he won't stay still*. Basil? Still life? I don't think so.

At first it was Basil from memory, then from photographs. I plan to do him in oils one day and frame him in a big shiny wiggly gilt frame.

I love art. I'm quiet then. I forget everything around except the picture I'm making. Basil is excellent for my observational drawing, as well as an audience for my flute performance practice. Basil is good to draw because he doesn't chatter or say, 'Ugh!' when he sees his portrait.

He is happy. Mona Basil. He wags his tail whatever you do to him. I've even done him in blue with one big eye. Picasso Basil.

Two seconds later Sarah leaped up and waved the paper under my nose.

Basil looked like a loo brush with a great huge grin.

'Erm . . . what are those, Sarah?' I asked, pointing at what looked like two big potatoes dangling from Basil's underneath.

'Those are his lumps!'

Of course. Silly me.

But from parental arguments I had overheard, I didn't think Basil would be joined on to those lumps much longer. My mother said they had to be Seen To by the vet. She said all dogs from the home had to be castrated. She said if the lumps in question stayed intact, there would be too many unwanted baby Basils wandering the streets. I could just see them, with little knapsacks on their backs, full of their worldly possessions . . . Oh! My father wailed about mutilation, female conspiracies and a dog's right to choose. I backed Dad on this one.

I wondered, What does Pram Gran's dog look like out of the pram? What is it called?

I love Basil.

Six o'clock. I slid out of my chair and crept off to the computer.

New messages?

None. My fingers itched to tappity-tap those keys and

write, 'Beautiful Craig. Give me the time and give me the place, PLEEEEESE!'

But all the wisdom, from friends, magazines, radio shows, television chats, even mothers as a very last resort, is, Be Ice Cool. Cooler than you ever want to be.

I controlled myself. I even got up and walked away from the computer.

So I had to revise instead.

muy buen

'¡*Buenos dias*!'

'¡*Hola*, M!'

'Morning Lizzie, morning Big Mouth,' called the Unspeakable who couldn't speak Spanish because his future astoundingly world-renowned career as global entrepreneur and international star required him to do German. Good, because that means he's not in my Spanish class.

We ignored him.

Anyway, what does he mean, Big Mouth? His mouth is much bigger and noisier than mine. It's like the M1 on a Monday morning.

'¿*Como la va*, M?'

'*No hablo mucho español*, Lizzie.'

Star turned round and said, 'You'll both be fine, really you will. You've done all right in your coursework, haven't you?'

Lizzie said, '*Si*. But what about the Craig mail, M? ¡*Es importante!*'

My heart sank slowly down the lift shaft. For the past couple of days it had been on the move all the time, never stopping for long.

'There were no e-mails from anyone last night. *No comprendo.*'

'Maybe he works long hours? After all, he's not at the bus stop every day, is he? He might work shifts or something.'

Bless you, Star. *That's* why there was no e-mail last night.

He wasn't at the bus stop. Was that a good sign or a bad sign for my Spanish exam? Maybe it would go well because I wasn't distracted by his gorgeous face?

Or maybe not seeing him was an awful omen . . .

What did it all mean?

'Don't be sad, M,' said Star. 'You'll hear from Craig again, I'm sure. And just think! Soon all the exams will be over.'

'No they won't. Why does time go so slowly? I just wish it would speed up.'

The Year Seven with the tuba *problemo* had plonked himself down next to Star again. Lizzie and I pulled faces at each other. This was becoming a habit. She'd be adopting him next.

Uh-oh! Snuffling noises.

'What's the matter?' Star asked him. She is weird! She's so shy and awkward, even with some people in our form but she was fine with Tuba Boy and his tears.

He spent a minute or so trying to control his gulping and snuffling and then hiccuped, 'I've – lost – *sniff* – my – book.'

'Which one?'

Sniffle snuffle. 'B-b-book for English. She'll kill me.'

'Just explain you've looked everywhere,' said Star gently. 'Everyone loses things sometimes. She can't kill you. She would be sacked and locked up.'

Tuba Boy cried, 'But sh-sh-she can't get no more.' His nose was streaming. Scabby yuk city. Star, you get the kindness prize. Just don't look at his sleeve . . .

'Which book is it?'

He wiped his nose on his blazer sleeve again. 'Book about a girl an' a boy an' snow an' ice and a big bear. It's – it's by W-W-W –'

'William Mayne,' said Star. 'It's brilliant. It's called *Drift*. I've got a copy at home. I'll bring it for you.'

It may have been a book about snow an' ice but I tell you, out came the sun on the Year Seven's face.

Hall of Horrors

I *hate* that exam hall. It's horrible. Usually I'm in there for nice things, drama and concerts and discos with all of us dancing.

Though there are PTA jumble sales. I try not to be there for PTA jumble sales. *So embarrassing.* My mother insists on helping. She makes me carry great huge bulging black bags of stuff she's cleared out from under the beds. The jumble sale smells of damp cardigans and dark armpits and people over thirty-five and abandoned shoes with mould up the toes.

But hear this! I would almost rather be at a PTA jumble sale than at exams when it turns into a Hall of Horrors. We trail inside and take our places for a couple of hours of hell. Exams are even scarier than the latest ride at Alton Towers.

When exams are over, they aren't really, because all you do is feel sick about the results.

The air crackles with sizzling nerves, rustling papers, and suspicion. Who's scribbling furiously when they swore they'd done no work at all and who's staring, lost-their-mind dumbstruck and gobsmacked? Is anyone weeping yet?

I hate that silence you get in exams. It's so lonely. I want to scream out *HELP ME SOMEONE! PANIC! PANIC ATTACK! BEAUTIFUL STRANGER RESCUE ME PRONTO!*

We didn't talk exams on the way home.

The Spanish exam? Over.

¿Malo? ¿Buen?

Dunno. *No lo se todavia.* TICK.

going up

'Emma! Emma!'

Sarah grabbed me round the knees and gazed up at me,

eyes shining. She was clutching a crumpled piece of paper.

'Basil got a gold star!' she cried.

I tried to smooth out the paper. Next to bog-brush Basil was a shiny gold star. Mrs Collins's print was rounded and regular as beads on a necklace. It said, 'Basil is beautiful, Sarah, and so is your work.'

'*Your* work!'

'Yes! All that writing I did!' she squeaked.

I see. All right, Sarah.

'Mrs Collins said I could bring it home. She said it's special. She said Mum would stick it on the wall.'

OK, I just wished I had a special new e-mail to print out and stick next to it.

'Look, Basil, look at your portrait!' cried Sarah. Basil sniffed the paper. He wagged his tail and looked at me, with small and puzzled eyes. Maybe he had hoped for garlic, or at least a spring onion.

Sophie wandered in. She snatched the paper from Sarah and wrinkled her nose.

'Is that supposed to be Basil?' she sniffed. 'Cos it looks like an anteater.'

Time to do a bit of revision, methinks.

'Emma? Emma!'

This time it was my dad. I must have fallen asleep over my maths. I like maths, actually. But I fell asleep.

'Emma! Your tea's ready!' hollered my dad.

And as I tumbled downstairs he said, 'Oh, by the way, you have an e-mail.'

Thank U 4 answering, Emma.
Can we meet up this weekend? I have a Saturday job.
Cum and see me. The big sports shop near the market.
Craig.
PS Good luck with your Xams.

My heart shot up to the Penthouse Suite, and on and on, right through the roof into the very sky! Why does everything happen altogether? Love and exams in the very same week, and no time to get the backs of my legs brown before Saturday, and maths in the middle . . .

We'll be there for you

But the first thing that Friday morning was the Real Steve.

He sat behind his wheel, smiling more than ever.

The second thing was feet.

No, not mine.

Jono Watkins' feet, because he sat behind me, with his leg wrenched up, almost hooked round his neck, sniffing his soles. Eugh! What *had* he stepped in? Not chewing gum.

He was trying to act cool, but his face was red. I noticed that he was scoring high on facial fuzz these days.

When Star got on I leaned forward and whispered, 'Jono Watkins has stepped in something. But *Steve Autentico* is *ici*. *¡Esto es maravilloso!* I can't wait to see Lizzie's face!'

We had a good cackle when we clocked Lizzie at

her *parada de autobus*, not knowing about the Steve Transformation yet!

Her face lit up as she clambered on, I saw her chattering away to Real Steve, smiling, and then – Thunder!

She flounced down the bus, snapped, 'Move over, M! I need a window seat after all that trauma. I don't ever want to ever ever see him at all.'

She pushed past, bottom in my face. Lizzie has a significant bottom.

'Been taking monkey glands, Lizzie?' guffawed the Unspeakable.

'Don't, Jono, please! My life is in ruins around me,' she cried.

'What's the matter, Lizzie?' I said. 'Real Steve is back, Lizzie. Stand-in-Steve has gone.'

'It's Real Steve plus Wife,' she snapped. 'He's only had time off to get married! He's got a gold wedding ring as well as an earring now! It is all over between us for ever. It's finally finished and my heart is broken into thousands of tiny fragments, never to be fixed.'

Silence for some seconds.

But I can't keep secrets, so I said, 'To cheer you up, Lizzie, I had an invitation. To meet up with Craig on Saturday morning in town.'

'That'll help a little,' breathed Lizzie, eyes shining with grief. 'We can shop.'

'I think Craig meant just me!' I squeaked.

'But we can come too, Star and me!' cried Lizzie.

'He doesn't have to know we're there.'

'I think he does, Lizzie,' frowned Star. 'I don't think we can hang around in the same shop and pretend we're not with M. We would keep looking, wouldn't we? Or phone you up. Even worse, we might giggle or point.'

Star is very wise sometimes.

'Anyway,' said Star, 'I'm working this Saturday, so I won't be able to come.'

'Oh. Shame. It would be such a LARF!' cried Lizzie. 'We could just watch from the shop doorway, and – and meet you after for a coffee in the Good Looking Café.'

Lizzie didn't mean the café was good looking. She meant the guys who worked there at the weekend. The sons, the nephews, the cousins five times removed. Lizzie could make a cappuccino last for hours while she eyed up their fathomless dark eyes, their Duplo Men arms in snow-white T-shirts, their tight black trousers and pert behinds.

'We'll be there for you, M,' she whispered so sincerely.

'You'll be there nosing,' I said. 'Lizzie, your idea is pants. Read my lips. NO!'

'On the very morning of my heartbreak, M!' she cried. 'How *could* you!'

She was doing the full tragic bit. She had an audience, Star and me, and the dreaded Jono Watkins. I glanced back. He was grinning. I made a point of doing great huge sniffs and the grin vanished.

Then I thought, careful, careful around Jono and feet . . .

That is a dark and dreadful skanky secret.

flasherless

Tuba Boy, *sin* tuba, was talking to somebody at the Mst. Imp. Bus Stop at the V. Cntr. of the Uni., an older boy, but the reason for the bus stop's Most Importance wasn't there.

The older boy shoved TB towards the bus just in time. He was a bit of a dreamer, that boy. I suppose you can dream at that age. You haven't got the stresses and strains you have when you're sixteen.

Why does Time go so fast? If only it would slow right down, I could be a Year Seven still, carefree, without exams, well, the really horrible ones that parents really nag about. I would also be without shameful foot secrets. My feet have a Past.

Ow! Don't you step on my old school shoes!

'I'm so sorry,' said Boss Woman and she patted my shoulder.

Good job I wasn't in my weekend foot-gear with my toes open to the skies and special nail art. Aagh! Her heels were true stilettos! It's a wonder I wasn't pinned to the ground. She was without the glossy tights. Tanned, smooth legs, no stubble in sight. I bet *she* never stepped in dog muck.

She was wearing great huge black sunglasses. On the bus! Was she famous? I don't think so.

Boss Woman picked her way carefully off at her stop, Genghis Khan in high-heeled sandals.

I suddenly realised she hadn't been wearing the blue flashers!

The Ring Fairy must have repossessed it.

Buddha, rescue my heart, why don't you!

*Hi M I am electronic now and I wanna hear all about
it as soon as it's happened!*
Lizziexxxxx

Sorry I have flu. Maybe sum other time?
Craig

My heart crashed down into the basement. It would never
get up again.

I could not cope alone with the Craig disaster. I needed
to talk. E-mail was no comfort in such a situation, so at
one second past six I phoned heart-broken Lizzie, who
was watching the Simpsons with a bowl of strawberries
and Toffee Nut Explosion, and making ever such a noise
down the phone.

Lizzie came over. She could stay. (We usually stayed at
my place because of Lizzie's annoying brother and his
friends. Sometimes they went off to Scout camp out in the
wilds to roar and wrestle and eat baked beans, and then we
could stay there but tonight they were all at Lizzie's.)

It was a simple matter to clear my floor and shove it all
under my bed. (I always did this for a big sleepover, then
there was room for lots of us, always Lizzie and Star and
often Amy and Francesca and JoJo and Carly too. It's a bit
like logs on the river, because the floor is packed with
figures in sleeping bags and Basil picking his way across.)

'Let's ring Star and ask her over too,' I said.

I could hear lots of shrieking and laughing near the phone. The step things had got their friends round.

Star was out, they said. Still at work, I suppose, in her old folks' tea rooms. Overtime?

We never stay at Star's these days. We did once ages ago when her mum and dad were still together, but nowadays I don't think she's allowed to have her friends round. Or maybe she doesn't ask? It must be really strange. I would be so lonely, I mean, she doesn't even have a Basil figure in her life.

Lizzie and I talked and talked. I explained how my heart was in the basement. Lizzie put her hand to her forehead and sighed for about ten seconds. She whispered that she had plumbed the depths of despair this last couple of days.

She said, Craig and I had cheered her up, but now that he couldn't meet me she was extra-sorrowful.

She said that she had been praying to Jesus, Mary and Buddha that she would get over Steve the Bus.

'Buddha looks all jolly and kind,' she said. 'I think he could be more help than Mary. And he looks a lot more fun than Jesus, as if he likes a good night out.'

I said, 'Buddha is not a personal god. I'm not sure he grants wishes. But if he does, let him rescue my heart from the basement, Lizzie, and put it back up high where it rightfully belongs.'

She said, 'Wow, M, that's really good! You should write a song. What about writing one for Jono's band?'

'You must be joking!' I spat.

'But M, you could play your flute in the middle,' she cried, 'and I could sing in a tiny black top!'

'You like being on stage, Lizzie. I don't. The only time I am on stage is in a bad dream. Hey, that reminds me, how are the career plans going?'

She said that she had finally worn her mother down. If she did well in music and drama and her other exams she could go to stage school for the next two years. George the Patriarch didn't like the sound of that. He had been shouting that he would be surrounded by loud women when Michael goes off to university and stage school would just make Lizzie worse.

'You're lucky, Lizzie,' I said. 'You know you want to jump about on a stage in front of people. And Star will go off to university and be so clever she will stay there for ever and ever.'

'And she'll marry a brilliant professor man with lace-up shoes and have lots of brilliant kids –'

'And they'll all be odd, but nice. But Lizzie, I don't know what I'm going to do, ever. I'll have to do a job and I don't know what it is! Everyone else knows what they want to do, except me!'

'I'm hungry,' said Lizzie.

PANIC! LATE NIGHT NOODLE CALAMITY! My mother had failed in her supermarket duties. There was no red Szechuan sauce. Can you believe it? We had to double up on soy sauce instead. That night I just hadn't the heart to make 11 o'Clock Chocolate Cake. I was too traumatised, deeply shocked and gutted, and we were missing Star. We had to settle for a tub of banoffee ice-cream.

We woke early in the morning at half past ten, feeling sick and gasping for water.

Oh well. That's too much soy sauce for you.

Monday misery

'How was it, M?' asked Star.

'Oh. Skanky. Work and telly.'

'No. I mean, how did your meeting with your true love go? In the sports shop?'

'It didn't. He had flu. Said he had, anyway. We rang you, Star. Didn't they tell you?'

'No. They never do,' she said. She looked down at her hands and blinked fast. Then she took a deep breath and said, 'I'm really sorry you couldn't meet him. And you should believe in him, M. Do you really think he'd bother to contact you in the first place if he was just going to pretend to be ill?' Star was being so sympo, all soft voice and a little worried frown puckering her forehead, that she made me want to cry, because you see I was beginning to think she'd got troubles of her own. She said, 'He took a lot of trouble to get in touch with you. How did he get your e-mail address?'

'I've been wondering that. Perhaps he knows someone

at school. My address was in the school paper when I was helping with those shoe boxes of Christmas orphan stuff. How was your weekend, Star?'

She pulled a little face. 'It was traumatic. I got into such trouble at work. I gave old Mrs Somercoates an almond slice. That was a serious mistake. She can only gnaw. She gets the almonds stuck in between her teeth and gets upset. And I gave her usual tea cake to Alfred who wolfed it down and then there was a dreadful scene because there were no more tea cakes.' She sighed. 'But Violet and Mrs Blake stuck up for me, even though I did their eggs for too long. They said, "These are like bullets, duck!" The boss told me off in front of the whole café. He says I'm too dreamy and living in my own little world.'

Well. Yes.

Lizzie's stop. She had serious, pulled-back hair today, and a pale face, all ready for the convent. She held her head high, eyes brimming with hurt, ignoring *El marido Steve*.

'Are you feeling a little better today, M?' she asked.

'Bit. Are you?

'I'll get through it.' She sighed like the north wind.

I hardly dared look when we reached Craig's *parada de autobus*. He wasn't there. I suppose I was relieved. He must be ill after all!

'Who are you ogling today, Emma dear? Keanu Reeves? A Madagascan Hissing Cockroach?'

That Voice cut past my ear like a chainsaw.

'Certainly not you, Jono Watkins!' I snapped and then

Star said, 'Where *is* he? I mean the Year Seven. The one who bashes folk with his tuba.'

'Maybe he's missed the bus. Maybe he's ill too.'

Light dawned at last.

'Of course! It could be him who told Craig my e-mail address. It could be his brother. After all, they use the same bus stop. Mind you, there the similarity ends.'

'He was writing something when you were talking e-mails,' said Star. 'Maybe he passed on your address. Shame he's not here, because I've remembered that book.'

I thought, Star's eyes look pink and puffy.

'Are you all right, Star? Don't worry about the tea cakes,' I said, but she just turned away.

Hold on tight

Dodo splats it on with a great huge trowel

I don't know what was the matter with Dodo Donaldson.

Cath Ratcliffe once said she had seen Dodo Dollop wrapped round Miss Poynton from English, like a piece of clingfilm, near the alcohol department in Sainsbury's.

Cath Ratcliffe says a lot of things. She lies through her teeth. One day she's engaged, next she's going to be on *Blind Date*, then she's had a text message from Leonardo di Caprio, and a week later she's expecting twins. Any Cath Ratcliffe story is doubtful, especially a story of Dodo in lurve. As Lizzie says, 'What real woman would want Dodo and his jumpers?'

His jumpers are hand-knitted for tall members of the ape family, by their aunties and grannies. No self-respecting machine could ever knit such garments. They're all loopy and stretched and that's even before Dodo has been in them, I know because one Monday he was telling us it was the first time he had worn his jumper, one with turtles and palm trees. One fave jumper has 'Dancin' round the sun' in red on green with a big yellow blob in the middle like out of an infant's painting. (The blob is the sun, I guess. Oh Tragic Man Dodo.)

Dodo was different that Monday. He was not mopey. He had a cappuccino shirt, and *almost* all right trousers, not the usual baggy old grey things all weighed down with keys and half-started chocolate bars.

'Decent shirt, sir,' said Lizzie.

'Thank you, Lizzie,' he said, and he smiled. I repeat. He *smiled*!

'And the chuddies look good,' added the Unspeakable.

'Cheers, Jonathon!'

Oh, Dodo, how hip are you!

It was then we decided he'd had a haircut, because we could see his great huge ears go up with the smile. His hair was one length on top and all shaved up the back. It was an improvement, except for the ear exposure. Men's ears just go on getting bigger and bigger as they get older, don't they? My dad's do, they are getting like elephant's ears. Dodo's are pretty big to start with.

A bit of old mutton dressed as lamb, yes, or rather old ram dressed as lamb . . . but he *did* look smarter. Maybe the Head had nagged him? She did her pieces when that Australian supply came to school in his sarong with parrots. (Well it was *disgusting*! *Especially when he sat up on the stage*.)

Teachers are not supposed to look like vagrants, are they, but most of ours do, the men anyway. But how merry was Dodo that morning! Trouble is, sometimes he thinks he's funny.

He was ticking and signing away at his desk and suddenly he looked up and quipped, 'Twinkle! Eh?' He was looking at Star. She glanced up, bewildered.

'Twinkle twinkle, little Star! You're not very bright this morning. Not much of a diamond.' Star forced a small smile and then looked down at her book.

Then he called, 'Got your blue stockings on, Star?'

I saw the hurt way Star looked at him.

Horrid silence. Nobody quite knew what to do, but of course, Cath Ratcliffe had to shriek with laughter, really lay it on. I said, 'Leave her alone.'

She stopped. She said slyly, 'Swotty Botty Little Star!'

Lizzie snarled, 'Just cos you're thick as ten short planks there's no need to have a go at Star. She's got what you haven't. A brain!'

Cath Ratcliffe's face tightened up like a white fist. She was quiet for a bit, but I know Cath, I've known her since junior school, she waits just past the moment so you've dropped your guard. Sure enough a minute later she sidled past Star and hissed, 'Looking a bit paki today . . . bit mixed up, aren't we, skin wise?'

Have I explained that there are two Lizzies?

Drama Queen Lizzie loves the dramatic and loves being on stage all dramatic and showing off.

Real Girl Lizzie has her everyday life and also Believes In Things.

Sometimes you can't tell the two Lizzies apart. Sometimes they become one.

Lizzie said, so calm and reasonable, 'Why don't you talk about skin with me, Ratchild? Or with Joanne and Carly? *Hey, Jojo*! Cath wants to talk skin with you!'

Jojo and Carly grinned and Cath Ratcliffe went whiter than ever.

Star just stared towards her book.

A single big tear plopped down on to her page. She stumbled up out of her chair and rushed out of the room.

'You've done it now, sir,' said Jono Watkins.

'Oh dear,' cried Dodo, his moment of smiley confidence long gone. 'I hope she's not really upset.'

'I'd be upset if I was that weird!' crowed Cath Ratcliffe. 'I mean, look at her, wog hair, thin as a pin, with scrambled brains and a stupid name.'

'Scabwoman!' screamed Lizzie.

'Girls, please! Catherine! Elizabeth!' cried Dodo Dollop, waving his hands around as Lizzie and Cath faced each other, shoulders hunched, hands at the grabready. Lizzie's nails were long and strong and she'd always been good at opening things. Cath's were all bitten. Lizzie would win and the class was seething with excitement now with Jono Watkins bawling, 'Women wrestlers, Love 'em! WWF Scratchdown! Girly violence, what a turn on!' and the Wot Kin all going, 'Woo Woo Woo!'

'I'll find Star,' I said but just then she came back in and sat down.

'Well hello, *Amaryllis*,' said Ratcliffe softly.

A*

Star's name *is* Amaryllis. She was christened Amaryllis. Her mum had read it in some old poem somewhere. She was Amaryllis at primary school, she said, and it was all right there. But at our school, things began to get bad, and at home as well, I suppose. That's when she wanted no one to notice her.

'But an Amaryllis is a nice thing,' I remember telling her. 'I got my mum one in a box for Christmas. It was half price. She put it in the front window. It grew a great huge pink flower on a stalk like a triffid and everyone who went past on the street stared at it. They thought it was amazing! It didn't look real.'

Star just looked at me. She said, 'Can't you call me A? Like you?'

She meant, like I am M. All right, I know Emma doesn't start with M.

Then A somehow became Star, cos she always got A stars. I thought of that and I'm proud, because it suits her, it's special and she likes it.

I guess there will always be Cath Ratcliffes scuttling around wherever you go, especially if you're a bit out of the ordinary, like Star, but I felt cross with Dodo Dollop, laying it on with a trowel like that, not knowing when to stop teasing her about her brains. He was supposed to be her ally. I think Star is, what do you call it, *differently abled*, because she is so clever with her books and her poems. She needs her own special teacher.

Dodo shouldn't have teased her so hard. What was the matter with the man?

Now that the bad time was over, he smiled all oozily at Star and she smiled back, because she's not a sulker, and then Dodo looked pleased with himself when he'd no reason to be pleased at all!

Star opened her book and began to read.

Except for her blotchy face, you'd never have known she'd been upset. I sneaked a look at her, and I had a real pang. Star is vulnerable, more than me, more than Lizzie. I think of that pearl hiding in the oyster shell and imagine someone's great huge foot crunching it to pieces.

scrub and pummel, why don't you!

What can I say about the next few days? I had to enter the e-mails in *The Daily Sightings*. Otherwise life was far from fun. The high point of the day was the post-exam TICK.

Life is hard when you are in love and having exams.

So to get me through these days of difficulty, I decided to spend some time with my feet.

First, a soak in peppermint soak stuff. Basil licked it off. Resoak.

Next, a scrub with deodorising exfoliating moisturising stuff. Basil as above, with sneezing. Rescrub.

Follow up with a pummel with lemongrass pummel stuff. *Mmmm!* Basil wrinkled nose and declined to lick.

On with the turquoise toe-dividers. On with Today's Varnish Choice — alternate Violet Cream and Morello Cherry.

Basil had to be banished at this stage. Basil sticks his nose to my toes and dabs with his skanky paw and the smudges have to be fixed with remover and repainting.

After Basil banishment I noticed — FOOF! — a bad bad smell, even though the foot cosmetics were so fruity-herby-healthy.

Basil had tucked his garlic bulb down the toe of my shoe for safe keeping.

Request stop

Life changes all the time, doesn't it? You never know who's waiting to get on at the next stop.

That Friday afternoon, Star had stayed in the library, Lizzie had just got off the bus, and *I* was gawping through the window feeling end-of-the-week, post-exam stress, trauma, nothing, stuff – when I saw *him*! That angel hair, that happiness halo, that beacon of light and so beautifully cut – unmistakable! He is better, quite better, and standing at a request stop. Well, my request is, get on my bus this minute! Never mind the e-mails, come and sit next to me!

Hot Breath, Hammering Heart – but squeal and wriggle and beam out LURVE as I might, he just wouldn't turn and look and the bus did not stop.

It wasn't until I was home that I knew what I should have done. I should have rung that bell. *Get off the bus, girl, get off and accost!*

I watched the little film in my head, the film that starred

the beautiful Craig and me. Next Friday I would be
PREPARED. Star was right, he must be interested because
of the e-mails. I would alight so innocent and so lovely in
that very street, with perfectly chipless toenails – I'd take
best sexy sandals, maybe some new ones, to change into on
the bus – ask him the way, offer him a blackcurrant boot-
lace, trip him up, anything.

But as it turned out, at that point of time, at the end of
the day, there was no need for me to jump off the bus next
Friday BECAUSE . . .

> *Hi M! Better now. Can we meet up this Sat morn?*
> *Tomorrow. Best time for me is about 10 when shop is*
> *not busy – is that 2 urly 4 U?*
> *Craig*

Freedom ticket

is this *moi*?

Wow! Wow! Wow! My heart shot back up through the roof and on to the Penthouse Suite! Isn't time strange? I saw him when he must have already already e-mailed me.

Then I thought, *meet* at ten o'clock? I have to tell you that on a normal Saturday I am not downstairs with the honey nut squiggles and the telly until at least half past eleven.

Ten o'clock in the sports shop *was* almost 2 urly 4 me. Craig had made no allowance for make-up time. I would have to get up at eight. On a Saturday! But we were meeting at last to fix a proper date.

'What?' shrieked Lizzie. 'That's far too early! I can't make it by then!'

'He's not making arrangements for two, Lizzie. It's me he's meeting.'

'I know! But we'll have to come to see what happens. Eleven's a good time. You will still look a bit fresh and tidy. All right, Star? Tomorrow at eleven in the Good Looking Café?'

I thought, we're meeting to fix a proper date at last!

I wished life would slow down. I wanted that morning to last for ever. It felt like a dream. Was this really me, oh so cool and casual, explaining to my mother that I was early because I was calling in on someone at work, someone who had seen me on the bus and asked me out? (This certainly was me, through the front door fast before she could draw breath to ask for details.) Was this really me, M Peek, getting the bus to town to meet The Beautiful Stranger who wouldn't be strange any more? Was this me, walking along the road to the sports shop? Was this me, shouting into my mobile at Lizzie when she rang to see what I had decided to wear?

Was this me, I, *moi*, hovering in the door way, hardly daring to go in? Better wait, better make it five past, ten past ten, mustn't seem too keen.

Oh no . . . one of my Morello Cherries is flaking. I hope Craig doesn't drop something and bend down and see it.

I couldn't see him. Beautiful Blond Craig. I couldn't see him anywhere.

Surely he would see *me* and come over?

'Excuse me,' I said to the brown-haired guy on the till. 'Um – is Craig in today?'

He looked puzzled. 'Yes,' he said. 'I'm Craig. Um – who are you?'

froth and whoosh at the Good Looking Café

I muttered, 'Mistaken identity, sorry, mix-up,' and dashed for the Good Looking Café.

He must have thought I was well bonkers, but how could I tell him the whole story? I slowed down. I'd seen that Craig before, but I couldn't think where. And the truly terrible thing was, *he* looked disappointed too.

Lizzie was in full make-up and pout.

'Lizzie, you're such a flirt!' I cried. 'I thought Steve the Bus had broken your heart?'

'He did,' she said. 'That was on Tuesday. Today is Saturday. Where is Star? Lost again? She's been here a few times now.'

'I drew her a map this time. A simple map of the centre of town, and I put nice turquoise arrows down the roads she was to take with STAR THIS WAY written along them.'

Star cannot do directions, but a moment later she appeared in the doorway, looking round for us and Lizzie and I stood up and cheered. She came flapping over and cried, 'I nearly managed it! I only had to ask once.'

'Who did you ask?' said Lizzie sternly.

'Oh – a nice man at the bus station. He said he'd walk me here if I liked.'

Lizzie hid her face in her hands and I said, 'Star. Don't go asking nice men. Please. Sit down.'

The Good Looking Café was full. Most of the customers were female. There was singing, there always is in the GLC. Shut your eyes and you can't decide if you're at a football match or the opera. You're at neither. You're at the Good Looking Café. It's *Nessun Dorma*, *O Sole Mio*, *Jailhouse Rock*, *Chicago you wonderful old man's town*. You know the kind of thing.

'So tell me what happened with beautiful Craig, M?' asked Star.

I took a great huge breath. I had to tell them. 'He wasn't Craig. It was all a mix-up. In the sports shop. He wasn't him and I wasn't me. Neither of us were looking for each other. He wasn't the Craig I wanted and I don't know who he thought he was meeting but it wasn't me.'

'Oh dear. I'm so sorry,' said Star. 'Listen to these wonderful arias, M. Give yourself up to the singing. Music can help to heal, can't it?'

'Not as much as a chocolate milkshake,' I said. Mind you, the throbbing arias or whatever they were did help. So much feeling and pulsating passion! The Good Looking dads and cousins and uncles were in full voice this Saturday as they frothed cappuccino and dribbled espresso. I listened to their great huge emotional warbling and watched their wobbling *whooshes* of hair, midnight-black.

And then there was Great Uncle Roberto. He was something else.

background notes on Great Uncle Roberto, Grand Master of Tiramisu

I first glimpsed Great Uncle Roberto through the display of mozzarella and tomato rolls. I saw his hair. It was a tidal wave of silver blue. Had it been helped, like those old American presidents, with the contents of a packet? Who can say.

Great Uncle Roberto always sat at the back counter, chopping. He chopped cheese and tomato and green herby bits. He put them in crusty rolls (yummy white ones with sesame seeds on top). He grated chocolate and crunched those almondy amaretti biscuits and blobbed out liqueur and cracked some eggs and whizzed creamy things in a whizzer and mmmm! it smelled wonderful and GUR sloshed it into trays which a younger Good Looking stashed in the deep freeze, because I don't think GUR was that bendy-supple any more.

'That's tiramisu in the trays,' said Lizzie authoritatively.

'Lizzie, I know about tiramisu,' I yawned. 'It's got chocolate in it!'

Sometimes Great Uncle Roberto burst into song, always on a high note, no build-up. This was a shock if you happened to be standing just near the counter. You could be ogling an egg mayo roll and all of a sudden an ear-splitting screech of Italian shattered your dreams.

dark espresso eyes

The only Good Looking who didn't burst into song all the time was the one Lizzie was interested in, Good Looking the Youngest. He had cropped black hair and eyes deep with soul, dark as espresso. He didn't have to sing to get attention.

Lizzie whispered, 'I will be here for a large cappuccino every morning of my life.'

She looked up at him all coy from under her thickly mascaraed lashes.

Good Looking the Youngest sauntered over to us, smiling all hunky-monkey, and placed a gold-rimmed plate before Lizzie. On it were three of those little amaretti biscuits, wrapped in pretty pink paper. Never talking her eyes from his, Lizzie unwrapped the biscuits and popped them into her mouth. Good Looking the Youngest returned to the counter and lolled and smouldered.

'Thanks, Lizzie,' I said. 'I counted three biscuits. And I count three of us.'

'You don't like almond, M, and amaretti is almondy liqueur,' she said through a mouthful of biscuit. She was right. Almond is about the only foody thing I don't long for.

'*I* do,' said Star. 'I love almond.'

Grudgingly Lizzie picked up the little twists of paper and emptied their crumbs into Star's hand. I waited for my milkshake, feeling all deepest sorrowful and sad. Only when I was about five and my Christmas magic wings and wand set wouldn't turn a bar of soap into chocolate was I so disappointed and let down.

'How will I ever meet him?' I wailed. 'He looks for me in the mornings, I know he does.'

'He might not be able to see you very well from the pavement. He might not know what you really look like.'

'Thanks, Lizzie!'

'Of course he can see you and he thinks you look good!' cried Star, putting her hand on my shoulder. 'That's why he has contacted you. There's just been some kind of muddle. Craig is a popular name now, after all. Perhaps there are lots of them.'

A great huge glass of milkshake arrived and not before time. I sucked it all up from the bottom with my straw like those council men with their leaf blowers in autumn. I felt calmer and less deepest sorrowful.

'Star,' I said, carefully, 'are *you* all right now?'

'I'm fine,' she said, staring steadily into my eyes. She did look better this morning.

I pounced on a last little bit of froth and sucked hard. There! Even Basil could not have found more. I said, 'Dodo and Cath were so stupid to you yesterday, Star. There's something up with Dodo at the moment, he's behaving really oddly.'

'Oh,' sighed Star, and made a little smile. 'I suppose I'm odd too. I'm not good at people. You two cope so well. You're not frightened of anyone, Lizzie. Lizzie Lionheart! And you, M, you are courageous, I mean, Jono teases you all the time but you don't let it matter. He fires little arrows but they just fall off. Both of you seem so – so well planted. You know, like lovely trees swaying in the wind, but still safe. I don't feel as if I have proper roots. Does that sound mad?'

'It sounds, er, different, Star, but I think I understand,' I said, although she made me sound so cool about the Unspeakable and I am not. 'Star, you have got a mum and a dad . . .'

'Yes . . . it's just I don't quite know where I should be. Everyone thought I'd flourish with Dad in the new family, but I feel all wispy and insubstantial. I feel too much on my own.' She shrugged. 'I suppose that's silly.'

'No it isn't. I mean, everyone's on their own, and you – you're just you.'

I didn't really know what to say. There's on your own and *on your own*. So I put my arm round her and said, 'You're different from a lot of people, Star. And that's all right!'

'Let's all be different from Cath Ratcliffe, PLEASE!' wailed Lizzie, hand to brow.

'There are good times coming. The sixth form will be amazing! You'll love it!' Aaagh! I sounded like my mother. 'Have you decided on your subjects?'

She hesitated, just enough for me to notice. Then she said, 'History, English, Spanish, maybe psychology. Maybe law. How about you, M?'

'*I* don't know! I don't know what I'm good for. I'll do

anything I get a good grade in. Or maybe I'll leave when I've failed everything. Oh Star, you know you'll go to university and be ever so clever! You know your future. You're so lucky!'

Star just shrugged. Later on that summer I remembered what I had said and felt like a traitor.

All pretty girls like lemon cake

'I'm going to get a job,' cried Lizzie, who hadn't really been listening to us. '*That* job there.' Her eyes were fastened like bolts on a notice which read *PART-TIMER NEEDED FOR WEEKEND WORK.*

'Just think of it . . . Good Looking the Youngest all day long!' she breathed. 'Hey, you two, we could all work here! That would be great, wouldn't it?'

'Lizzie, they don't want three people. They only want one,' I said.

'And I work every other Saturday in the tea rooms,' said Star. 'I'm better with the old ladies and the scones. I don't think I could cope with the singing and the trousers here. And it's nice to have a Saturday off and doss around with you two.'

'Yeah, we don't do it often enough,' I said. 'Tell you what! My house. Tonight. 11 o'Clock Chocolate Cake?'

'I'll be there,' said Lizzie.

'I wouldn't miss it for the world,' cried Star.

Another Good Looking appeared and smiled a smile

googly enough to melt a heart of reinforced concrete. It nearly melted mine, and I prefer blondes! In the middle of our table, next to the single pink carnation in its wiggly silver candlabra-stalk-holder-thing, he put a small basket full of cakes. The cakes were gnome size and drenched in lemon syrup.

'All pretty girls like lemon cakes,' he murmured.

That should be embroidered on a sampler and hung up on the wall. Quotes from *The Wisdom of the Good Lookings:*

All pretty girls like lemon cakes.

These three girls do, anyway.

We did a quick reccy of the shops to see if there was anything new and decent. I checked on the supreme black jacket I looked at every week. (And I'm still looking at it. My mother won't buy it for me. She's a minging meany. She says a hundred pounds is too much, but what does money matter! Her generation is so materialistic.)

Star whispered, 'Hey, do you think I would be all right in these? I've got tea room money.' She was stroking a pair of silky turquoise trousers.

Lizzie pawed through the rack of trousers like Basil after a beetle. She snatched out a pair and said, 'These will fit you, annoyingly skinny girl. Go and try them on.'

She looked fantastic! Star is thin, all right, but she has a waist like a wasp and a flat flat tummy. 'Immaculate, Star!' screeched Lizzie.

'Get a top too,' I told her.

She got one in the same zingy turquoise. She brightened right up! Lately she's looked a bit drab mustard but with the turquoise, and happy, she was clear honey. She bought some tiny blue and silver ear-studs.

'*FWAWF!*' screeched Lizzie, flapping her hand in front of her nose. 'The shops don't half stink in June.'

'It's not the shops,' said Star. 'It's the armpits. They build up into a hot impenetrable fug, don't they?'

'Impenny what? Star, you're weird!' I said. 'Let's get out of here. I know! Let's go to the park.'

the ice-cream park

We never went to the park these days.

When I was little I went all the time and when I was a bit bigger I got lumbered with the sisters. Once. Sophie pushed the roundabout too fast for Sarah to get on, and then Sarah tried to drag Sophie off her swing, or was it the other way round? They screamed at each other for a very long time on a very top note with hands at the grabready and mumsy-looking folk kept tutting. Never again.

It was only two stops on the bus.

We ran towards the swings with our arms out behind us like Concorde. Lizzie and Star don't scream like my sisters and all three of us managed to get on one swing, Star sitting and Lizzie and I standing like storks, one foot on the seat, clinging on to the rope.

'Uh-oh!' said Lizzie. 'Here comes a Percy Park Keeper. Do you think we'll pass for twelve?'

We waved and smiled at the keeper stomping towards us, but his face didn't change so we knew he wasn't having any so we got off and sauntered away.

'Hey! Look over there,' said Lizzie.

A row of forlorn deckchairs faced the bandstand. Parked by them was an old pram.

'C'mon, you women!' cried Lizzie and we charged over.

There sat Pram Gran in her deckchair, legs almost too far apart, eating ice-cream. Something was in the chair next to her. In the dip of the canvas we saw her little brown and white dog. Curly hair. Grey muzzle, so much older than Basil. No back legs.

He wagged his tail so that it thumped on the canvas.

'What a dear little dog. What's his name?' asked Star.

'Trotter,' said Pram Gran. She held out her ice-cream to the dog who licked it daintily as if he had ice-cream every day of his life.

I think perhaps he did.

'I save him the chocolate flake till last,' said Pram Gran.

I thought, no hair net today. Her hair is as tatty as Worzel Gummidge's straw locks. I thought she'd have tight sausage curls under that pink hair net but she is truly unkempt. A wild, wild old woman.

'Couldn't he get one of those little trolleys for his back?' asked Star. 'Then he could run with his front legs.'

'I tried one, but he'd rather go by pram,' said Pram Gran. 'It's warmer for him too.'

'Do you bring him here every day, then?' I asked.

'Ooh no! We like variety, Trotter and I. We get bored by routine. You're supposed to like routine when you're getting older but we don't. We go down the market, up the shops, all over the place. We only come here on Saturday and Sunday. For the music. Trotter loves it. His favourites are Verdi and Puccini.'

'You should go to that café in the town centre,' I said. 'The men in there sing that sort of stuff all the time.'

'I don't think they'd like my dog in the café,' she said. 'He restricts me from many venues. But he's worth it. He is so small, but such wonderful company.'

She smiled up at us and I thought, she's been pretty, many decades ago. Her eyes are startling blue. She said, 'I know you young ones must think I'm bats.'

'Oh no!' we cried, too quickly.

She said, 'It's all right. You see, I'm on my own. Trotter is my life now.'

'Haven't you any children?' I asked, thinking too late, nosy Emma.

'No' said Pram Gran. 'I *was* married and we were very happy. We never wanted children.'

I nodded with perfect understanding, a picture of squabbling Sophie and Sarah in my head.

Pram said, 'My husband died suddenly. So I went to the dogs' home, and there was Trotter.'

'That must have been his lucky day,' said Star. She's always so good at saying the right thing. Trotter wagged his stumpy tail. He really was very sweet, but personally I preferred Basil.

flaked out

Well-loved, magical, off-key music rang out across the park.

'Make mine a 99!' cried Lizzie.

'What, even after all that stuff at the Good Lookings?' I said.

'But it's a special day,' she said. 'Here we are, the three of us in the park, and it's Saturday night at M's!'

She was so right, so right! We had a quick dance, sort of Givin' it Large, Strip the Willow, Round the old Maypole, with our ice-creams held high in celebration.

'You know, I don't think there is a brass band concert on a Saturday,' frowned Star. 'I think Pram Gran has got it wrong. I think the band plays on Sundays. I know, I'll leave them my chocolate flake to compensate.'

And she trotted back towards the bandstand. She held out the chocolate flake for Deckchair Dog to nibble. He was quite refined, turning his head delicately from side to side.

Basil would have had it in one.

'She's mad,' said Lizzie.

'Which one?' I asked.

chocolate wars

When I got back home I cleared my room. It looked amazing. You could even get to the curtains. Then I went to the kitchen to check chocolate cake supplies. Guess what?

'Sophie! Sarah! Who ate my chocolate!' I screeched.

They were in the sitting room, three inches from the telly. Sophie had recorded a programme about Embarrassing Illnesses. A man was holding up a big bottle with something sloshing about in the bottom.

'Where is it?' I shouted.

They turned to me. Sarah had the tip of her tongue up her nostril. It's the thing she does best. Sophie dived to switch off the video. She stuffed something in her pocket.

'Is that chocolate, Sophie?' I asked, all threatening.

She took whatever she'd hidden out of her pocket and placed it on top of the television. At once Sarah whinged, 'My dragon! Mine!'

'Yeah, well you don't love your silver dragon,' cried Sophie. 'I gave him to you for Christmas and all you do is hammer with him. You've broken his crest off and hurt his tail, look!'

'Mine! MINE!' screamed Sarah and went for Sophie, hands at the grabready.

'I know he's yours, *Stupid*, cos I gave him to you, but now I wish I hadn't cos you don't love him properly!' shouted Sophie.

'Sophie, remember she's the little one,' I said, thinking, I've heard that somewhere before. 'Let her have the dragon.'

'I *am* letting her have him,' she said. Then she rolled her eyes around in their sockets. That way she couldn't see me and so she thinks she is invisible. Sophie is strange.

'Do you know anything about chocolate?' I growled.

'Basil?' she tried.

'No, Sophie. You know and I know that Basil can't get a chair and reach up into the cupboard. Basil does garlic, not chocolate.'

'It isn't just you who likes chocolate, Emma,' said my mother from the doorway.

'Well I'm the only one who makes chocolate cake!'

'And then you eat it all while we're asleep!' wailed Sophie.

'And *you* eat the blackcurrant cheesecakes and leave me the minging strawberry one,' I countered. 'I have to make sacrifices just because I'm the eldest.'

My mother sighed her 'What-a-family-I've-got' sigh. Whose fault is that?

She went for her bag and rummaged for her purse.

'Here you are,' she said.

So Basil and I set off to Bottom Bobs.

And guess who I saw!

Well roody poo, it's –

Outside Bob's was a great huge car. It was pink and silver. It had wings. I don't mean real wings like an aeroplane or a bird, I mean jutty metal wing shapes coming out of the back. People were walking past it very slowly, pretending not to stare, because they are Oh so polite and respectable around where we live, but they are truly nosy on the sly.

One man was muttering about parking because the great huge car took up two spaces.

Basil dashed over to the car, almost strangling himself on his lead, and weed bigtime against the wheel. Basil has to make his mark sixteen or eighteen times in one walk to frighten off rivals because – I'm not sure, really. Small dog syndrome, perhaps.

I tied the lead around the dog post outside Bob's door. Basil had never liked that. He thought the post was for other dogs of less import. He whimpered piteously and it sounded like one of those curly blowers you get at kids, parties.

I hurried into Bottom Bob's and searched for chocolate. Three bars would do for a serious chocolate cake.

Bob's shoppers were turning heads towards a strange noise. Basil had stopped whimpering and was doing small wolf-howls of neglect and deprivation.

Back for two more bars – you can't be too careful. Supposing the sisters found them again? In the end I bought eight altogether, and a smaller bar in case I felt faint on the way back. Your minerals and things get depleted when you're sixteen, worn away through stress and ongoing menstrual business and having horrible exams, and chocolate is an important source of iron.

Then I saw him for the very first time. He was behind

the till. I knew it was him, because one of the ladies who serves in there called, 'Do you need more change, Mr Bob?'

Mr Bob!

'No thank you, Denise,' he said.

He was putting food into a carrier. Microwave dinners for one, I couldn't help but notice them, lone lamb hotpots and solitary toad in the hole, individual chicken curries and little steamed puddings you could pop in your microwave . . . I'm curious, I'm interested in those about me, maybe that horrible J-O-B word could involve being curious about my fellow folk? Private detective to the rich and famous? Interviewer for expensive magazine?

Jono Watkins says I'm the nosiest woman he knows but he has no taste or respect, no wit or wisdom, no S&S and his judgement is truly lacking in . . . judgement.

I wondered if there was a Mrs Bob left home alone this Saturday night? I narrowed my eyes so he wouldn't know I was looking, and I tell you Mr Bob had lots of gold rings, but not on his wedding finger. Who could we fix him up with? Pram Gran wheeled her pram into my thoughts . . .

He clacked – I say *clacked* because he was wearing patterny pointed-toe roody-poo cowboy boots – he *clacked* across to the door and put the carrier bag behind it, for later I suppose.

And then he returned, switched on a smile – *click* – and tapped all my bars into the till. I'd got the money ready anyway. I know about life, I know the price of a bar of good chocolate.

So did Mr Bob. He counted my money very carefully, every last penny, and I don't know why because Mr Bob was dripping gold, from top to bottom. As well as all the rings he had a thick gold chain at the neck and a gold watch. Well, if I'm truthful I could only see him down to the armpits because of the counter, but I think he was loaded.

And I tell you something else. Top Bob's top was not his own. That hair never grew out of that head. It was thick as a doormat, and unnaturally shiny. Mr Bob had bought it.

Well roody poo!

Basil goes social climbing

When I liberated Basil from the dog post he leaped at me as if I'd rescued him from the animal testing laboratory. Off we went down the street.

I stopped to open my chocolate. All of a sudden I felt the lead tighten and begin to vibrate.

That's why my mother keeps threatening Basil's potato lumps! Oh the shame oh the embarrassment, the PANIC! PANIC ATTACK!

I mean if it had been a *dog*! but Basil was wrapped round the leg of a woman, make-believing it was some dogette of his dreams. Worser, worst, oh very worst of worse, Basil's legs were clasped round *Boss Woman*!

She kept kicking out her leg, trying to shake him off. But Basil is a determined dog.

He would not let go.

Why did it have to be Boss Woman! Did Basil know how glamorous she was? Surely dogs look for different things in love situations, thick fur and wet noses or meaty smell, not Nina Ricci eau de toilette and oatmeal linen.

And why did Boss Woman always invite disaster? She got bashed by Tuba Boy and now her leg was being bonked by Randy Small Dog. I tried to turn my face away from her as I prised Basil off her leg. Cream linen trousers . . . well, they had been cream a minute earlier. Trouble is, Basil is a mud magnet.

'Sorry! Really sorry. He's only young,' I mumbled, thinking, does she recognise me out of uniform? She bent to flick mud and fur off her cream linen leg. She said, 'I think your little dog is confused. You'd better take him to one side and talk to him.'

Later I thought, she was trying to make me feel better by joking. At the time I just went double Szechuan as I dragged Basil home.

All around the houses

cool voice, calm manner

About an hour after I got home Sarah came to tell me I had a phone call.

'It wasn't a girl,' she said.

'Then who was it?' I shrieked. 'Didn't you take their name or number? What kind of receptionist would you make!'

She shrugged and ducked.

'Let me check the number!' I shouted, shoving her out of the way. She trotted after me to the phone and watched me dial 1471. I didn't recognise the number it came up with, but the caller was local. I muttered the number a few times and Sarah said helpfully, 'Oh, that was my friend Jane. She rang to ask me to go swimming. After the call for you, Emma, that I don't know who it was.'

Sisters! Who needs them?

I did a bit of history revision with a small part of my brain. I like history. We've done Northern Ireland. We've done the history of medicine. I like that (although you don't always want to know what they did to people, especially without any anaesthetic). In my book was a drawing of The Father of Medicine, Hippocrates. He was ever so like Sean Connery, you know, the old grey Scot who was a James Bond. He is your granny's Robbie Williams.

The phone rang again. I heard Sarah say, 'My mum says, "Please get off the face of the earth, and we don't want your guttering, thanks." Bye!'

A few minutes later it rang again. I beat her to it this time. *Cool voice, calm manner . . .*

Guess who it was?

'Hi, babe! Jono here!' he cried, cheerful as you like. He had no right to be cheerful.

'I'm having a party. Tonight. Can y'all come? You and the girlies?'

'It's a bit short notice, Jono!'

'I've only just decided,' he said. 'I'm gonna get the Wrinklies out of the way to watch a film. Nothing too scary or sexually explicit. I don't want to encourage heart problems. The party is at 22 Tasmania Road. Come about nine. Bring drink. I'm doing the food. It's sorted. See ya!' Click.

party party

'But of course I'm coming!' cried Lizzie. 'I am a true party animal!'

'Er – yes, I'll come if you two are going,' said Star doubtfully.

(I had to ring them to give advance warning, you see, so they could bring a change of clothes and make-up.)

In the meantime I concentrated hard on toenails representing the Milky Way and the night sky with as many moons and constellations as I could get on them.

I couldn't get all of it on. Really you had to look at the two feet together to get the full effect so I'd have to shuffle a lot.

Star and Lizzie were early for Party Preparation.

'Hair wash, then style!' cried Lizzie, barging past me and straight up the stairs.

With great self-control I decided not to use any of my mother's *Shampoo in the Light – Sunkissed Dawning*. It was for old grey hair after all. I thought, if something goes really wrong on the hair front, I'm not letting Jono Watkins be one of the first to see.

We washed each other's hair and conditioned and styled and scrunched. We had a go at Basil too but he ran away from the hair dryer.

We made each other up. It's great being made-up by someone else, isn't it? You really feel it makes a difference. I like make-up a lot sometimes, especially for parties. You can pretend to be someone else or re-invent yourself and be mysterious.

Lizzie makes up and she can become someone new! Lizzie goes for eyes. Tonight it was the Cleopatra look. I've never seen so much eyeliner as Lizzie lined with. Her pair looked like the big magic eyes they painted on the front of those Egyptian boats so they could see where they were sailing. She did big Blackcurrant Buffy lips. She was all in black as usual, all sheeny, and the effect was Ancient Egyptian prophetess with a mobile phone in a leopard case.

Star wore her turquoise trousers and top, and we did her hair so it looked like a lovely gold and black fern.

'Good hair, Star,' murmured Lizzie, smoothing the palm of her hand over Star's head.

'I may be getting it cut short,' she said. She didn't sound as if she wanted it cut at all.

'How would you have it done?' asked Lizzie, gently bouncing her palm on Star's springy topknot.

'It would be cut into a bob. Lynn said I should. At the same place as her and her kids.'

'But why?'

'Lynn thinks it's a bit Afro.'

Am I nosy? M for meddle and mix it? I said, 'I don't know why Lynn can't just let you be.'

'I think she wants me to look more like Dad and my hair is a bit of a giveaway,' said Star. 'I do look like Dad. My eyes are like his. Mum used to call them onyx eyes.'

I peered into her eyes. They were goldy-greeny-brown. Yes. My grandpa has an ashtray made of onyx and it was like Star's eyes.

'Your eyes need Stuff!' announced Lizzie, waving the mascara wand so that I thought she'd poke Star's eyes out.

She put on some gold shadow, all restrained and subtle (for Lizzie). Next we sprinkled glitter across Star's face so that her skin it looked like honey when it goes all gooey and crystalline in the jar. Star looks like no one else. She is different. She is understated. She is subtle.

Star stood up, all shy and pretty. She didn't know what to do with herself!

So she dithered about a bit, glancing at herself in the mirror, and then said, 'Ooh! I've brought lots of crisps.'

She trotted over to her bag and waved a big shiny packet at us. Sour cream and chive.

'I know they're Jono's favourite,' she said.

'Eugh!' I shouted. 'Think of his breath after that lot, Star!'

'And I've got cola and tonic,' cried Lizzie. 'They'll go with it!'

'Go with what?'

'Whatever!' said Lizzie in her you-are-an-eejit, M, voice.

I realised I hadn't got anything ready to take. Jono Watkins certainly wasn't getting chocolate cake. He might like it. I raided the cupboards and found roasted peanuts, some cans of lemonade shandy and some Cocktail Fancies – cute biscuits and wafers, all in little plastic cubicles. My mother bought them at Christmas. She always goes potty buying unsuitable stuff for parties when she never has any anyway. Her friends are all asleep by half past eight. She buys things 'just in case . . .'

Talk of the devil. My mother slouched past the doorway, muttering about wet towels.

She called, 'Don't you girls want something to eat before this party?'

'No,' I said.

'I think there will be nibbles there, Mrs Peek,' said Star.

'Hmmm . . . mind you behave yourselves, now,' said my mother with menace.

'We will, we will!' sang Lizzie the Liar.

Don't mothers go on about nothing.

'I'm not sure they should be going to a party in the middle of their exams,' called my dad, jealous because he never ever ever goes to any parties whatsoever.

Oh no, I thought, here comes a pincer attack from both parents but *SURPRISE MOVE BY MY MOTHER!* 'They need a bit of fun,' she said. 'The exams will be all the better for a break. Now, Emma, you know your dad will always come and collect you if it starts *to get late or anything*!' The warning lights were switched on in her eyes. Full beam.

'Mother,' I sighed, 'it's only Jono Watkins. He only lives just round the corner.'

I noticed that much of my dad's head shone white in the full light of the hall. Oh dear. Still, it might be worse, he might buy in a Mr Bob-type head warming wig.

Jono Watkins Land

Only just round the corner is a very long way in your high-heeled strappies. It's all around the houses. You have to take little tottery Chinese steps and have the Milky Way spangling across your toes. But we hardly *ever* get the chance to wear decent shoes because of school.

We tottered past the Jono Watkins bus stop. Funny to see it there all lonely, with no one waiting. I wonder if it feels different getting on there, with an extra bit of bussing. It's strange to think it exists there without us. *Mmmm . . . philosophical or what?*

Jono Watkins' house looked quite normal. It was white with some of those pretend-Tudor-William-Shakespeare-mansion-bits stuck on the front and Busy Lizzies in window boxes.

The door was opened by a devil, all in black.

Jono. Someone had painted white and black make-up all round his eyes and he had found something gooey to make his hair stick out in great huge spikes, like a porcupine.

Suppose he thought he looked like a pop star, sort of heavy metal devil, sort of Eminem meets Cradle of Filth, down at the graveyard with a chainsaw.

Well, Jono Watkins, I decline to comment!

He roared, 'Wow Star! You look terrific! Lizzie, you're luscious as ever!'

I waited. Nothing. Thanks.

'Oh, Jono, really! What are you like?!' I said, staring pointedly at his tattered soot-black top.

His smile faded, but only for a second. He said, 'I'm rock hard as always, an' tonight I'm vampiric black metal, Emma.'

Right. When he turned to go in, I saw that his waist and

bottom were hung about with chains. Do vampires wear chains?

There were LOADS of people, most of them in our year, some sixth formers, some big ones I didn't know, from Jono's scabby rugby team, I suppose, and then all his mob of friends and followers, guys and geeks. Ordinary, really.

You see, our school is a big huge ordinary state secondary in a sort of ordinary area. I mean, it's a bit of a mixture. Sort of suburban edges, not inner city, or trendy fashionable bits either. There aren't any real extremes. I mean, there's no one your parents wouldn't want you to know. No one dangerous. No one truly unsuitable. Shame.

'Come and see my buffet!' cried Jono Watkins, pushing us past a darkened room bursting with song from a woman with a hollering voice and a LISHP! and on into the kitchen.

'*Da-da*! he fanfared, waving his arms. 'My centrepiece!'

On the table in the middle was a great huge green melon, all hedgehogged up with pineapple and cheese on sticks. He'd also chucked a lot of shreds of salad on an enormous dish and strewn scarlet worms on the top.

'Chillies!' he cried, following my dumbfounded look. 'And I've stuffed them!'

'What with?' asked Lizzie suspiciously.

'Oh, garlic, little fishes from an old tin, more chillies and some black things I found in a jar . . . anything I could find really. I saw this dude cook it on television. But I am feeling innovative, and the crocodile is my own thang. Creation copyright. It's melon. You'd never guess, would you!' *Crocodile . . . Mmmm . . .*

I cast my eyes around the kitchen. I saw a big jar of gherkins in cloudy yellow liquid and a beer mug stashed full of twiglets.

'How very sixties, Jono,' I said.

'Glad you like it,' drawled JW. 'It's all my own work.'

I remembered Jono's own work. In Year Nine we cooked every other Friday. Jono made Deep Sea Fish Extravaganza and left it in the classroom all weekend. The cleaner thought there was a dead body. I suppose there was, really.

One week we made scones. There was a feud. Jono said his family was from Yorkshire way back and they called them SKONS.

Alexandra Parker (who is a wealthy bimbette who lives in a great huge house with electric gates and a carp pond) (I don't know why she doesn't go to Benedean Ladies or somewhere rich instead of our school) (but she's nice) anyway, she said, 'OH NO! They are sc-OH-ns.'

I'd never really thought about it. What's in a name? You just cut them in half and eat them with butter. Jono's skons were all his very own, as you can see.

JONO WATKINS' SKANKY SKONS

(This is a basic recipe with Unspeakable variations)

You will need:
- **225g self-raising flour**
- **lump of butter (40–50g)**
- **tiny bit of baking powder**
- **tiny bit of salt**
- **bigger bit of milk**
- **some currants. Jono soaked his in something first . . .**

1. Rub butter and flour and salt and powder till crumbly.
2. Add some milk. Add currants if you like them. Jono added sugar too and goodness knows what else.
3. Roll it out on a floury board – not too thick, not too thin.
4. Cut out scones with a big flutey cutter, if you're normal. Put on greased-up tray. Brush with milk and\or prinkle flour on tops.
4. If you are Jono Watkins you make one big huge SKON, sprinkle cheese round the top edge for hair, make eyes and a great big grin with the currants (self-portrait) and eat it all yourself.
5. Bake them hot, 7 or 220°C for about 12 minutes till golden and toppled. *OVEN GLOVE ALERT.*

Eat them warm with jam, clotted cream, honey, butter or chocolate spread.

There were no Skanky Skons on the menu tonight.

Jono thought he was doing cool dude food, but he was like a little kid doing a Blue Peter thing. He needed help on the food front. Why didn't we eat before we came, as I had suggested?

I said, 'And for dessert, Jono?'

He wasn't giving in. 'Over there, M!' he cried.

On a curling cardboard plate sat fat slabs of yellow and pink Battenberg cake with little squiggles of that aerosol cream. 'Garnished by *moi*, Emma! And plenty of pollies!

Too right. Casting my eyes all over the place once more I saw wobbling towers of polystyrene cups. Bottles stood in ranks on the table and the windowsill. He'd bought the cheapest crisps in the supermarket, you know, those cheapo economy ones all thin and mustardy. He had made dips. Garlic and chilli. FWAWF! Tomato ketchup. Salad cream with black dots in it. Something thin and green.

Jono Watkins was studying me with his mouth full of twiglets, so he looked like a squid. I hated him studying all my faults. I could feel Szechuan sauce red creeping up my neck. He was staring at my nose, wasn't he, thinking, bunny rabbit.

I said, 'What's your problem, Jonathan?'

He stuffed in his twiglet tentacles, crunched and then spluttered 'I have no problem at all, Emma. I was just thinking that you look quite tasty.' He sniffed the air in an affected manner. 'And you smell good too.'

I glared at him and at once he looked down, staring pointedly at my feet. Was he studying the Milky Way spangling my toenails? Was that why he was doing his 'look at me looking at your feet' stare?

Or was there another reason . . .

When I was in Year Seven I was innocent and naive

When I was in Year Seven I was innocent and naive. I know that's hard to believe now.

I went to a party. There were boys. At junior school we'd grown out of boys at parties, but now they were back again.

I felt really awkward. I hadn't got my two really good friends then. Lizzie scared me. She was so confident even then. I love Lizzie but she's like a bollard. You can't get past her. Lizzie will stand up to anyone and that's a bit scary when you're in Year Seven, until you realise you are the same sort of girl.

I didn't really know Star – she takes a long time to know – and she hadn't been invited anyway.

At the party I wanted to hide in a corner but I felt as if a spotlight was following me, to show me up. I was all awkward.

We had videos to watch, chosen for us, as you do when you're tweeny. I perched on the edge of a sofa. The video ended. People drifted out into the kitchen. I stayed sitting on my sofa. Across from me was a scabby old cushion on a chair, all white and moth-eaten. I went to grab it and it spat at me and hissed and went back to sleep. I could smell its old fish breath.

It was hot. I took off my trainers. I didn't really know much about trainers then. I didn't understand them. I didn't know how they work.

I *certainly* didn't know how they can smell.

Jono Watkins was also in Year Seven. Guess what? He was truly irritating. He was tall even then but he had a funny voice because it was breaking. His hair was wild and orange, he had dyed it, so it looked like Van Gogh's sunflowers in a strong wind. He wore his boxers pulled up above his trouser waistband, all the boys did then. He kept singing this song, the one about mammals doing hormone things on Discovery Channel programmes.

SCATHE!

Anyway, Jono Watkins came crashing into this little room where I sat on the edge of the sofa with my trainers off. The old cat was still asleep on the chair, purring.

Jono glanced at me, glanced away, and then back again.

And then he waved his hand in front of his nose, went, 'FW*AWF*! FW*AWF*! Chemical warfare in here!' and crashed out again.

secrets, shame, humiliation and chemical warfare in my tender years

It was my feet, wasn't it! *Humiliation.*

Oh, I wanted the ground to open and swallow me up, but not before I'd got my trainers back on and laced up tight to keep in the smell.

I spent the rest of that afternoon terrified he'd tell everybody that my feet smelled (like that horrible cheese my dad eats, sort of dark yellow and collapsed that smells like Dracula's bedroom, and is a cause of Dad's sulks if my mother doesn't get it from the shops, but she says it's embarrassing if you don't go straight home because people look at you and wrinkle their noses).

I don't think Jono Watkins could have broadcast to the world about my feet that afternoon, because every time I saw him after that he was eating. He's always been greedy, but he stays thin, which is utterly unspeakable. However, since that party there have been years and years for him to tell everybody my shame and humiliation.

I soon 'lost' those stinky-poo trainers.

'You think I'm made of money!' cried my mother when I told her. 'How can you lose a pair of trainers, Emma? Where are they?'

'Dunno.'

And to this very day I dunno. I dunno where the dustbin men took them. They were stuffed inside an empty Cheerios packet, and then inside the black dustbin bag. After that, I just dunno.

We'd never mentioned feet, Jono Watkins and I, but I always think he is in full possession of my smelly secret and might shame me in front of millions!

Get your foot on the bottom rung of the evolutionary ladder

The first hour of Jono's party went ever so slowly, mostly talking and eating and crushing pollies and throwing cocktail sticks.

And then it speeded up. The faces were whooshing round me. All Jono's cronies were there, The Wot Kin, featuring Polite Adam who smiles all the time, Glowering Ashad playing the cynic and hoping everyone would notice his new trainers, Dean and Luke, Scott who's far too clever for his own good and Tunde in gold-rimmed glasses who is just so *serious*. I'm fond of them all I suppose, but they're such little *boys*. I even knew Adam, Luke and Ashad at primary school.

'It's hard when you mature early,' I said to Lizzie. 'Boys just never seem to get higher than the bottom rung of the evolutionary ladder.'

'I know,' she sighed. 'I find it well nigh impossible to relate to my male contemporaries. I don't like to make gender judgements, but they seem so loud and crass and immature. *Oi! Tunde! Chuck us a bit of that stripey cake!*'

I saw that the pink and yellow cake had been prepared much, much earlier. All yellow oily stuff had soaked into the cardboard plate, and the squirty cream had collapsed and sort of separated. I nibbled thoughtfully on a pineapple chunk. It was dry and tough, way past its sell-by date. I stood in a corner, all pensive with pineapple, and realised I was looking for just one face – *HIM*.

Not transferable

Chunky monkey

HIM. The one who wasn't called Craig after all. Yes, I knew he wouldn't be there at the party but things were getting a bit surreal and if you are really stuck on someone, you can't just transfer your feelings, can you, like a ticket, just cos you are at a party given by some goon in your form. Cath Ratcliffe arrived under a great huge slick of make-up. She was all held in by sequins and she had great huge goth boots on her broomstick legs. Her boobs were all squidged together in a sort of black housefly top, and she had shaded in a cleavage that nobody had ever seen before. It looked as if the Knocker Sprite had visited her with a box of felt-tip pens.

I couldn't believe it! Jono Watkins was hanging round her, grinning and topping up her polly. Awful thought . . . had he done the demonic bit, the son of Frankenstein's monster makeover, especially for her?

Lizzie dived for pineapple chunks and then sallied forth and took the bottle off Jono. She shot Cath a look like a sharpened stake through a werewolf – or is it a fork? or a silver bullet? golden chopstick?

Whatever it was, it didn't slay Cath Ratcliffe.

'More, M?' shrieked Lizzie, waving the bottle dangerously.

'No,' I said. I felt a bit funny. I emptied my polly insides into Mrs Watkins' Busy Lizzies. That should perk them up.

'Pineapple on a spear? Good for vitamin C,' cried Lizzie. 'Hey! Will you look at those arms!' I followed her gaze. Boyd McKenna, Year Thirteen. His face was a bit bland and some rugby pitch plastic surgeon had redesigned his nose for him but the rest was a decent shape.

'He got that nose in the scrum,' said Lizzie knowledgeably.

I suppose the arms were good if you like muscles. He'd put body oil on them. A wasp buzzed around him hopefully. He had a little white T-shirt to show off his bronze bulges. Chunky monkey! Lizzie sidled up to enchant him. Huh!

It was getting so noisy. The rugby boys were shouting and doing stupid donkey laughs. Jono Watkins was leering at Ratchild and she *loved* it. He was slouched against the units, roaring, 'BRINGID AWN!' and, 'ORRR RAT! DAWNMISSMIUP, ENNIBADDY!'

I translate for those of you without a degree in Jono Watkins Speak: 'BRING IT ON. ALL RIGHT. DON'T MESS ME UP, ANYBODY.'

Cool, I don't think.

Star was sipping orange juice and looking frightened.

'I don't think I like parties, M,' she said.

'How many have you been to?'

'One,' she said. 'This one. I don't really get asked. And even if I do, I can't get there because I lose my nerve about going on my own.'

'Sorted, Star! When it's parties, you come with Lizzie and me and then back to my place to stay. You'll be fine! I know it's difficult for you to have us back. It really doesn't matter.'

'It does,' she said. 'I feel bad about it.'

'Have you asked your dad about it?'

'Not really.'

'Why not?'

She wouldn't look at me properly. She said, 'He's always talking to someone else.'

'But you're his daughter, Star.'

'Not that you'd know. I don't look much like him.' She gave an odd little laugh. 'I'm not the same colour as any of them. They are all so white. Whatever that means. Last night Katy came and leaned her arm on the table next to mine. Hers is white as milk and it made mine a cappuccino. She just smiled at me, sort of triumphant. They make me feel I don't fit in.'

'You're like your mum.'

'And that's fine, but she's not here, and I suppose Dad didn't know what he was getting when he married her and they had me. Now I think he is ashamed of me. He puts a space between us. It's like a river with currents you can't see from the bank. I can't get across it.'

All this time Star's face was turned away from me as she fiddled with polystyrene cups and plates.

'But Star, you're special. And you're happy at school. Aren't you?'

'Ye-es.' She didn't sound too sure. Then she brightened up. 'At least people notice me at school sometimes. I don't want it to end. I'm a ghost at home. A shade they don't want to acknowledge. Their eyes slide past me.'

'What about your — what's she called? Lynn?'

'She's busy. They're all very busy. You know, if I ask for the salt they sort of shunt it round the table until the last one leaves it just where I can reach it. They get drinks for everyone except me. They think I am different.'

'Yeah, well you are, Star! That's why we love you so much!'

'No, I mean they really think I am odd. They don't like to talk to me. Because I'd rather read than watch telly, and . . .'

Something big barged between us, something with great huge feet, shouting, 'C'mon, Star, let's dance!'

Star recoiled, shaking her head, she obviously didn't want to dance, with Jono or ENNYBADDY else, but he's just so insensitive! He steered her out of the kitchen and into the big loud music.

I'll say one thing for Jono Watkins — but only one — he has good sounds.

His party sounds were different — Stereophonics, the

Red Hot Chillies, Macy Gray and Moloko, and Moby. So many good things start with M, have you noticed that?

Jono liked his music loud. A black man with a cavern deep voice was singing *I'm gonna work now, baby*! That's what it sounded like, anyway.

You should see Jono's dancing! He was flailing around Star like a great huge happy octopus so that she lost her fear and just had to giggle and dance back.

brake failure

From then on it was downhill all the way. The brakes did not work.

Lizzie skipped in leading Boyd McKenna by the hand. And then someone went, 'Dunce?' right in my ear. It was that sixth former who grunts. I think he's called Matt. He smelled of sweet hair gel and beer and smoke.

We danced next to Lizzie who was shouting, 'And after drama school, the West End stage. That's in London, you know, Boyd. Then maybe a screen test for Dreamworks. There are lots of actors I want to work with.'

Boyd McKenna's mouth was even more open than usual. He grunted, 'Really? Who?'

'Maybe Cruise, maybe di Caprio, or Jude Law. I'd consider them,' said Lizzie generously.

I snorted with laughter. She looked at me, held my gaze with her wide dark eyes, challenging me. Not a blink, not a blush. That's Lizzie!

I know the truth, and she knows I know. Maybe that's why we're such good friends.

But Boyd McKenna just stared at her with his jaw trailing like a lovesick moose.

The Unspeakable crashed over and turned the volume right up, then seconds later flailed up to me and waved a bottle.

'No, no, no!' I said.

'Huh. M for Mouldy Fig!' he cried. 'Like shome, Lishie?'

'Yes!' she screamed.

Sundays excepted

back to nature

It couldn't really be after twelve, could it? I peered at my watch, it was all blurry but I didn't remember getting it wet. Sunday already?

I went for a wander. Jono Watkins' stairs were a bit uneven. I tried the loo. It was already locked, the bathroom too. I peeped round the door of one bedroom – all neat with frilly curtains and an ensuite with one of those low basins for washing your feet. Must be the parents' room, I didn't feel I could use their ensuite, I don't really know why. I could wait . . .

I saw Jono's room – aaagh! But the door was wide open and the lights were on (in Jono's case that usually happens but there's no one at home!). He had rude posters of women with big chests.

Bottles of deodorant and hair stuff and I don't know what else were lined up on his table like little armies ready for battle. Well, they'd lost.

I needed greenery for my soul. I needed leaves and calm but not as much as I needed the loo. The bathroom one was free now, WING YIP! Wonderful. Some things are worth waiting for.

Those stairs really were a bit swimmy, and there was a smell of smoke wafting up them, POUF! FWAWF!

I found greenery for my soul. Mrs Watkins had a conservatory. It was all new and smart, in a Jono house too! There were big plants and a pot thing with holes, with herbs poking out. I brushed against one that smelled like cat wee. I can't remember what it's called . . . Mrs Watkins also had a set of that cane furniture that makes red criss-cross marks on your bottom. It had bright carefree cushions. My mother covets cane furniture with carefree cushions, but we can't have any, because Basil would chomp the legs and do things to the cushions.

But in this conservatory I saw something bad propped against the wall.

The Unspeakable's guitar! And there was Ashad's drum-kit! Waiting . . . I had already noticed that the Watkins had a small piano. Tunde played piano, Beethoven, Bach, jazz and rock, anything. He called it, 'Tickling the Politically Incorrect Ivories'.

I bet Luke had brought his saxophone. And now I remembered. That Matt played bass guitar.

That could only mean one thing.

Jono's group would be playing later.

That was why Jono had dead Pharaoh eyeliner, dangly chains and black lips.

Last year the lads consulted Lizzie, Star and me about names for the group. We came up with some brilliant suggestions – Sequin, The Kin, Bad Boys Band, Drop It . . . quite a variety for them to choose from. They totally ignored us!

They call themselves *Mass Devastation*.

I picked my way back to the action. The volume of the laddos was turned up maximo. All I could see was pollies passing between bottles and mouths and all I could hear were braying sounds. That Matt lunged at me. I thought he was wanting to refill my polly.

No. I had a horror close-up of great huge slobbery lips, old Mick Jagger with implants. Nightmare Yuk! Wet plasticene. It was like being snogged by a Puffer Fish off the sea bottom in a David Attenborough programme.

I was out of there fast. I found Star in the kitchen, tidying up empty bottles and crushed pollies and bits of Monster Munch, scooping them neatly into empty cans. Oh Star!

She said, 'Actually, M, I want to go now. Can I borrow your key?'

The Unspeakable pushed past me. He was leading – oh my god – he was leading Ratchild by the hand. She shot me such a smug look, like a vampire at supper time.

Lizzie swept over to the table and tore out more pineapple spikes from the crocodile.

'Like them Lizzie?' cried the Unspeakable. 'I think I'll be a TV chef. Lots of money there, you know. I'll be seen preparing food in the midst of my cool, busy life, on the rugby field, in the kitchen with the mates and babes all watching.'

'I hope your taste in food is better than your taste in females,' snarled Someone.

Silence.

Then I said firmly, 'Lizzie, we're going. Star and I have had enough and you certainly have!'

'Oooo-whoooh!!' she shrieked. 'Bossy old M!'

'Just let me put these out of the way,' said Star, bottles under one arm. She turned the handle of a door. Nothing. She wrenched away at it, but she's a bit clumsy is Star, and I said, 'You're probably turning it the wrong way. Here, let me –'

'It's locked,' she frowned. 'I think it's the utility room.'

And then the door opened from the inside.

'Oh. I'm so sorry,' said Star. A pair of hands reached for the bottles.

I had to have a look.

Mr and Mrs Watkins were camping out in the utility room. Well, it must have been Mr and Mrs Watkins, unless Jono was renting it out to some other old couple in there. They'd got the telly and the DVD player. I heard warbling. Unmistakable trilling. *The hills are alive . . . with the sound of MEW-ZIK*! I spied a tray with mugs, a teapot and a packet of biscuits. (They were Hobnobs. I know my chocolate.)

Saturday night, and the wrinklies sure know how to have fun. Poor old things. So much for Jono treating them to a might out at the cinema. Tight-wallet Watkins.

We stumbled to the front door.

I noticed that the Unspeakable One had dumped squidged-up Ratchild in a corner somewhere and was draped around Alexandra Parker.

He is such a gold-digger!

The return of the Killer Pineapple

'*And* they had schleeping bags in there,' insisted Lizzie as we tottered down the path.

I could hear Jono's music blaring out around the neighbourhood. I wondered if his neighbours liked Skunk Anansi. They're excellent, but Skin's diction is clear as crystal and her lyrics are not what you would want your parents to hear. They would be unable to cope.

'Something is ringing,' I said.

Lizzie sat down on the pavement. 'Where's my phone, M?' she cried.

'How should I know?'

She emptied her bag and slapped her purse to her ear. 'Hello?' she shouted.

Star knelt by her and felt through all the stuff on the pavement.

'Here it is,' she said.

'Hey up, Boyd!' shrieked Lizzie. 'Boyd Smirnoff, are you

missing me? I'm on the pavement. No, Boyd. I don't wanna check out Jono's greenhouse with you. I wanna to go home now.'

She cancelled Boyd and stuffed everything back into her bag.

'Amaretti biscuit, anyone?' she said, waving little packages of crumbs. 'Or a lemon cake case? Yum, still sticky . . .'

I sat down to eat my crumbs. I stared at the dark shapes that were my feet. They were cold in my strappies. In my jacket pocket I found gloves from the winter. I pulled them on over the sandals. I got up, dragging Lizzie up with me. She made such a fuss. Star took her other arm and we tottered home.

It took a very long time. We seemed to zigzag and Lizzie kept sitting down and singing, 'Say my name Say my name' – it was the only bit of the song she could remember.

In the end I snapped, 'It's Lizzie Astopoulis! Lizzie Astopoulis!! Lizzie Astopoulis! There, I've said it, now will you please shut up.'

Star doubled up, shaking and giggling. I don't think I've ever seen her laugh like that and it was great, it took my grump clean away.

'Thought we were doing chocolate cake, M!' shouted Lizzie as she fell on to my front door. I could hear Basil yapping ferociously to repel burglars.

'Lizzie, it's midnight and you've woken up the dog and there's probably no chocolate left!' I cried, rummaging for my key.

Panic over. There sat the chocolate on the shelf. They hadn't eaten it after all, or if they had, my mother had dashed Bobwards before he shut up shop to drive home to his lonely microwave.

I began to break it up into little bits, ready to melt, tripped and banged my bottom on the units, *ow*! It was Basil's fault. He was sniffing round my feet hoping for stray chocolate fragments. I realised I still had on the gloves so I sat on the floor to pull them off. Basil growled and wagged his tail. This was a great game. He grabbed the gloves and growled and tugged. Didn't matter now. The gloves had big holes in them anyway, where my heels had been. They were ruined, as tattered as Jono's T-shirt.

'Jono likes your feet, M,' said Star. 'He kept looking at them when we were dancing.'

Slight PANIC! PANIC ATTACK!

'Jono Watkins likes Cath Ratcliffe,' I spat.

'He's all right, you know, M,' she said. 'He's shy. That's why he's so noisy. Shyness gets people different ways.'

'Shy? PAH! He's humungous, tasteless, insensitive and SO LOUD!' I sat up. A light was thinking about dawning or shining or something like that. 'Do you fancy him, Star?'

'No, of course I don't. He's just a friend. But he's kind and he makes me laugh.'

'You can say that again.'

'He makes me laugh. Anyway, M, what about That Matt?

'Eugh! Lips of cod! It's not been an evening of great romance, has it? Unless you think you've fallen in love, Lizzie. Lizzie?'

Lizzie had gone very quiet.

'So is it all off with the Good Lookings and on with Boy Boyd, Lizzie?'

No reply.

Star whispered 'M . . . maybe chocolate cake isn't such a good idea after all . . .'

Lizzie pulled herself up by a chair and stumbled across the room towards the sink. So at twenty-five past one we cancelled 11 o'Clock Chocolate Cake.

I turned on the taps hard before my mother could see the pineapple chunks.

Sunday Syndrome, all forlorn

By two o'clock on Sunday afternoon, Lizzie and Star were gone.

Sunday can be the exception, the odd day out, can't it? I was definitely suffering from Sunday Syndrome, all forlorn.

My heart was stuck just under the ground floor and it couldn't make it back up again.

What is life all about? My friends had gone home, there was no romance, only exams and the thought of one of Dodo's little 'sharing' talks on Monday morning, something like, '*My* form won't let me down! The best grades in the year, the most passes. We've got bets on it in the staffroom, you know. On form, my form? Ha! Ha! Ha!'

And what am I going to do? What word has three letters and begins with J? Would the parents still support me when I'm twenty-four? Would they still keep me in chocolate?

I can't imagine being twenty-four! It is so very old.

'Emma, you're overtired, that's all,' said my mother when I declined her offer of me tidying up our breakfast stuff. Parents. What is their purpose? What are they *for*?

I worked out another revision timetable in emerald green and gold, fitting subjects around the best TV. You've got to have breaks, haven't you? Otherwise you get even more Syndromes.

So there I was, tired, friendless and lovesick with chipped varnish on my toenails and a headache. My family was dysfunctional. My sisters were fighting over a geriatric Barbie doll which Sophie had stuffed into a dog food tin and hidden in the rubbish bin. My mother kept apologising to the tumbler-dryer. My father was shouting obscenities at the lawnmower. They had been rowing about the dog's future. The lump situation wasn't looking good from Basil's point of view.

The only happy being was Basil, all unsuspecting. He had spent the night of his dreams, with three big girls who loved him. Two of them slept in sleeping bags. Basil likes to burrow in sleeping bags. When he gets too hot he just boings out and up on to my feet.

Now he sat on my knee, facing me, a bit like a meercat. Have you ever read a book called *The Hobbit*! *The Hobbit* was a sort of hairy dwarf-thing with hairy toes. Basil has Hobbits' feet, with long tufts of orange hair between his toes. I don't know if Hobbits' feet smell as bad as Basil's do. He's also got a wobbly dewclaw toe on each ankle. I think that may mean he is gifted, or blessed with magical powers in some way, like the seventh son of the seventh son. Basil probably is a seventh son of a seventh son, at least, with all sorts in his extended family. My mother says the vet will take the wobbly dewclaws off under anaesthetic when he – ugh! I can't bear to think about it.

Basil looked up at me with small, earnest eyes. He has a wisdom without words.

'Will I ever really meet Craig Who Isn't?' I asked Basil. 'My Blond Bombshell, my Beautiful Stranger . . . and what am I going to do out there in the world? What is my J word, Basil?'

Basil gazed at me. He just didn't know.

There was a rapping on my door.

Take the middle way

the middle road

My mother doesn't do rapping. She does an 'I am a polite and mature woman' tap.

So was it an exciting visitor? No, it was Sophie. She wandered in, without being asked. I was about to shout her out when I saw the quivering lip.

Sophie doesn't cry. Does she? Yes, it seems she does. She wiped her nose with the back of her hand and wiped her hand on her jeans. She turned towards me and I saw her face was angry.

'What on earth is the matter?' I snapped. Sophie isn't the little one, that's Sarah.

Sophie gets into trouble at school for being lippy. That's what her teacher told my mother. She said Sophie had attitude. I looked at her face, all jutty and defiant. *Hmmm.*

She growled, 'Sarah didn't ask. She just took it. Took Barbie. 'Snot hers.'

Sigh. 'Sophie, she's little, you haven't played with Barbies for years, you say they're stupid.' (I think Ken's gay anyway, so why does Barbie bother?)

'Sarah gets everything!' she screeched. 'She didn't ask f'rit! Sarah gets new Barbie dolls and even Ken but she has to have mine too!'

The lip quivered. The floodgates opened. She sobbed great huge painful sobs. She just stood there, all wooden, with tears streaming down her cheeks. Basil kept jumping up to try and lick them. He loves cleaning up salty tears. I thought how dramatically and totally someone like Lizzie flings themselves into crying, she really enjoys it, but Sophie just couldn't deal with it. She hated the attention and people might think she was weak if she cried. She was all racked with it, all unhappy and d'you know it made me feel a bit upset!

I said, 'We need to take the Middle Way, Sophie.'

I didn't really know what the Middle Way was, but I'm always hearing people talking about it, so I thought, that's a bit safer than the left or the right. Anyway, the thought of the Middle Way slowed Sophie's sobbing right down. It *must* be the right way to go.

M for mediator

I looked at snuffling Sophie and thought, I don't know my sister very well.

I said, 'Where is this ancient Barbie, Sophie? Where have you hidden her?'

Lip tremble. She wasn't going to tell me. Sophie is so different from Sarah. Sarah often sits on my knee, even if Basil is already there. She asks for help with homework, she asks to play games and to go to the cinema. Sarah is easy. Sarah finds life simple, I think. She's sweet and pretty and she doesn't need to do confrontation.

Oh dear.

'Just want her to ask f'rit,' muttered Sophie. Fair enough.

'Yes, but where is it? I'll get Sarah to grovel – I mean, ask – but I have to have the Barbie first, Sophie. Where have you stashed her? You haven't broken more bits off, have you?'

Silence.

Then, ''Sin the dustbin.' This sounded strangely familiar. ''Sin a Basil tin. Help me, Emma.'

Yuk. Sophie had squidged old Barbie into an empty dog food tin, one of those tall ones my mother buys to save money, except it doesn't because when I serve Basil's supper he gets really big helpings which may be why the vet says he is too roly-poly-portly and needs to go on a diet.

So guess who had to sneak out and rescue Barbie although I detest the whole Barbie nation. Guess who had to wash traces of smelly dog food out of her yellow hair and off her salmon-pink limbs.

Then I had to negotiate. I found Sarah confiding in Ken, whispering just below his bouffant, telling him her nasty middle sister had kidnapped his new girlfriend.

'Come with me and we'll sort it!' I said, all decisive.

There were two dodgy and highly dramatic moments. First, I thought Sarah was never going to say please. Second, she kept mouthing it so that Sophie couldn't actually hear it.

And then Sophie snapped, 'Trade!'

Sarah's face went all cunning. She ran to her room. She came back. She offered a hair ribbon, a sparkly slide, a photo of a boy band, an old Harry Potter book with the cover missing. She knew quite well that Sophie didn't want any of them. Worth a try, though.

'How much do you want old Barbie, Sarah?' I asked.

'Very, very ever so much!' she cried, eyes as big as minidiscs.

'Do you want her as much as . . . a dragon?'

Sarah froze. I knew I was there!

'Aw right,' she muttered. Head down, she went to fetch the little dragon with the broken crest. M for mediator? I had sorted the Barbie dispute in true stateswoman fashion.

Maybe a high-flying job — sorry, career — in international relations, up there with Kofi Annan, is what I should be looking at, *with power suits and embassies and sleek, stretch limos and hand-made chocolate . . .*

Miserable Monday

The phone went at five past seven.

'Emma!' groaned my father, bald bit glimmering in the

early dawn light, 'it's your insomniac friend on the phone.'

It was Lizzie, wanting to know what exam we had that day. Honestly. She's so dizzy and forgetful sometimes.

'Lizzie, you're so dizzy and forgetful sometimes,' I told her.

'Thanks, M!' she snapped.

When we were little Year Sevens and Eights Lizzie was always on the phone first thing. She was ringing for homework or ingredients. She never remembered what we were cooking. I'd hear her shouting ingredients at her mother. If it was something unusual that wasn't in the Astopoulis store-cupboard I had to take in two lots. I'm quite together in the forward-planning department, where food is concerned, anyway.

And then I thought of Star. She often missed the bus on cooking days because she had to shop for her stuff on the way to school. Your parents should do that, shouldn't they?

At least, my sisters were happier this morning. I found myself looking at Sophie and thinking, maybe it *isn't* easy being the middle one, espesh when the youngest is all charming.

AND IT ISN'T EASY BEING THE ELDEST, EITHER!!!! with exams and a love object who won't get on your bus.

To make it worse the bus was a bit early and I had to run which made me cross.

I was not going to look at the Unspeakable.

I looked down the bus, looking everywhere else but at

Jono Watkins. I stubbed my toe. I sat down and filed through the books in my school bag. I told myself that it wouldn't be long until Friday and I could jump off the bus and snare the Beautiful Stranger.

'Enjoy the party, M? It went on till four o'clock, babe. Devastation played a great sesh. Somebody came round to say they didn't like the music! Can ya believe it? They said they were getting the police. Can ya creddid it? An' they moaned about us playing football. Well, it was my mum's old cake tin. She didn't mind . . .'

Pause. I think in his daydreams Jono was still at the party.

He said, 'Y'know, we artists and musicians an' that have always had problems being accepted by mainstream society.'

Another pause.

'Were you sick, M? Did you chuck up, babe?'

'No, Jono, of course I did not chuck up!'

'Oh. Lots of people did!' he crowed. 'You should see our lounge carpet. We could do with an industrial cleaner.'

'Thank you for sharing that with me, Jono. You say the sweetest things.'

More pause.

'Why are you so cross, Emma? Tell me?"

'I AM NOT CROSS JONATHAN! I HAVE HAD SIBLING TRAUMA! IT IS MONDAY MORNING WITH EXAMS! I AM TIRED! SHUDDUP!'

He went, 'Not a happy bunny, then, M?'

Bunny? How does he know . . .

'Hey! How did ya like my mate Matt?'

'That Matt? Not much.'

'Oh! Thought you'd fallen for him bigtime!'

Ignore him. He'd just have to give up. I stared hard out of the window. I could hear him singing away to himself, imagining a sea of adoring female faces before him as he played his guitar, but at least he wasn't pestering me.

Star got on. Before her bottom had even found the seat he called, 'I couldn't fix you up with anyone on Saturday night, then, Star?'

'No, Jono, you couldn't. But it was a good party and the food was delicious.'

'Thank you, Star. I'm glad someone appreciates me!'

Star was white-lying. I was seething.

He said, 'I have to say I feel sorry for you females now I've seen things from your corner. It took me ages to get my make-up off after Saturday. It was a real learning curve, as they say.'

I sneaked a look, narrowing my eyes so he wouldn't catch me spying, and there was certainly still a vampiric smudgy look about him.

I said, 'You put on too much bat stuff, Jono.'

He said, 'It wasn't me. It was my mum. You don't think I'd do make-up, do you? Sounds pervy to me.'

And then to Lizzie it was, 'Whey–hey! How's Boyo Boyd?'

'How should I know, Jono?' she said. 'But thanks for the party. When's the next one?'

Was she serious?

He was.

'Oh, in August I guess. Sort of summer celebration. Maybe a barbecue? Burgers and sweetcorn and tofu for the veggies? I know where to get cheap ketchup, buckets of the stuff.'

'TV chefs don't use ketchup, Jono,' I said. 'Goodnight. Now, Lizzie, what are you going to do if you see Boyd?'

She put on her Lizzie-is-deep-in-thought face.

She said, 'On Saturday night I fancied Boyd Smirnoff. But I don't fancy him in Real Life. Know what I mean?'

'No,' said Star and I as One.

'Let me explain, girls.' (Lizzie was now Bridget Jones.) 'At the party Boy Boyd looked good with his chunky muscles and all. But he's not very bright. He really is just a pretty face.'

'Lizzie, his face is all bashed about!'

'Just a pretty arm, then. Good bulges.'

'So you're still in love with Good Looking the Youngest?'

'Don't know. You see, since my heart was broken by *him up there*' (daggers look at Steve the Bus) 'I am treading very carefully along the Romance Road.'

'I suppose you didn't find the man of your dreams, either, Star?'

'Well no, M. But then, I don't suppose there is a man for me.'

She gave a wry little smile.

'Oh, Star, that's rubbish. You looked terrific Saturday night. There was nobody suitable. For *any* of us. And you're just a bit shy, that's all.'

Silence.

I said, 'We're not having much luck on the Romance Road, are we?'

nunnery notes

Star said, 'Perhaps we'd better go and live in a nunnery. You know, like in *Hamlet* when Hamlet tells Ophelia, "*Get thee to a nunnery*"?'

'You mean we could go and live in a convent?' mused Lizzie. 'We'd look good in black and white floaty robes. Nuns can look cool.'

'I don't think they wore those black and white habits in Shakespeare's day,' said Star.

'We wouldn't be in Shakespeare's day. We'd be in Now! But there are disadvantages. Nuns have to eat roots and soup all the time and they don't have central heating or go shopping. I haven't seen them buying ice-cream in the park.'

'And they don't have dogs' I said.

Gloom. I think it's No to the Nunnery for now.

We had reached the Most Important Bus Stop at the

Very Centre of the Universe. Tuba Boy shuffled into sight, but no Beautiful Stranger.

And then we saw, something we never expected to see.

Pram Gran. Alone.

She was wandering along the pavement with her arms sort of stretched out either side of her as if she didn't know what to do with them.

She had no pram to push!

'Oh no,' whispered Star.

'What'll she *do*?' wailed Lizzie.

Poor Pram Gran. Now she had no one.

What if anything happened to Basil? Who would be my friend and confidant? Who would listen to my favourite tracks over and over again without moaning? Who would hide his garlic in my shoe?

heart attack

It could only get worse. Middle Way? Now we were on the Low Road.

At school, Cath Ratcliffe was making doe-eyes at Jono. She had so much stuff on her face, she looked as if she worked on the ground floor of Debenhams. Why doesn't *her* mother jump out at the bottom of the stairs and witter on about, 'You've got years and years to wear make-up, you're not supposed to wear it for school.'

To make things worse, Dodo was prime-time cheerful.

There we were, his thirty responsibilities, stressed and

skin-troubled from lack of sleep and stamina-sustaining chocolate, wondering whether to buy shares in Spot Dots, worried about World Peace held in the clammy hands of Bush and Bin Liner, anxious about our D minuses and A stars and lack of Beautiful Strangers, and all he could do was smile. Heartless Dodo! Is he unnatural, or what? So now we had him to worry about, too.

Lizzie was building up to a performance, I could tell. She was breathing quickly, and bending her knees as if she felt weak. She shot me a quick and calculating look which said, Tell on me and you're dead, M.

'Mr Donaldson . . . I've been having some pain on the bus,' she said in a tiny little voice.

'Keep cool and calm and just do your best, Elizabeth,' he said. 'Life will not be ruined if you get a B instead of an A.'

'It will–if–I–get–D!' wailed Lizzie. 'Then they won't let me go to stage school, and I really really want to.'

'Elizabeth, I know your parents. All they want is your happiness,' sang Dodo.

'Chees-ey!' roared the Unspeakable and I have to say he was right although I would never let him know that in a million billion zillion years.

'But sir, I have pain. It's the stress!' whispered Lizzie, placing her hand on her chest and rolling her great huge eyes.

'Wrong side!' boomed the Unspeakable One. 'Your heart is on the left, love!' and then he had to back towards the door, helpless with laughter, as Lizzie advanced at the grabready, throwing Lennox Lewis punches, shouting, 'I'll finish you, you Jono Watkins, you and your pineapple chunks!'

Ratchild crowed, 'See? You can't act your way out of everything, Elizabeth Astopoulos!'

'Wanna bet?' cried Lizzie.

There was a long moment of silence. Lizzie is always prattling on about timing. She put it into practice now. She toppled backwards on to a chair, clutching her throat, eyes rolling. But even Lizzie couldn't keep it up for long and she burst out laughing like a hyena.

We fell about. Lizzie's 'heart attack' and the pummelling of the Unspeakable was real therapy. We all felt a bit better.

Dodo was right for once. No one would die if they didn't get their grades, no matter what their parents threatened. I've never heard of GCSE results being a motive for teenagericide. They are just marks on a paper in some overpaid Suit's office. That's what Mr Benson in maths says, anyway.

Then Carly burst into tears. She was leaving, you see. Quite a few people were. Carly is going to a college to do stuff they don't do at school. Some of us were actually going out to work! Seven were going to a different sixth form.

We felt choked. We'd been together for five years! One by one we joined in, even Ratchild. Dodo was sent out for tissues.

You never know who's at the next stop

But life goes on and you don't know who's at the next bus stop, or if the bus is coming, or even if there will be three of them together.

And now here was another unexpected life event, an invitation!

Alexandra Parker, her with the sc–OH–ns, goes, 'Oh yah, you lot, Friday, you're all invited to my place about seven. For a pool party. Till nine or half past, and a bit of a barby too!'

Wow! Pool party and a bit of a barby too. Just what we need. Friday, eh?

'Alexandra,' I whispered when I hoped no one could hear. 'If – er – please can I bring someone? Although I don't know if he'll be able to come.'

'Sure. The pool is vast!' she shrieked so that Jono turned and looked. Wouldn't he just! And I wonder who he will dive-bomb, Alexandra or Ratchild?

Wow. I can't wait for Friday, although I wish I had more

tan to show off in my bikini . . . and then after that, there are weeks and weeks of worthwhile things, like chatting and shopping and eating lemon cake and blackcurrant bootlaces.

'It'll be great to go to a party on Friday won't it?' I said to Star on the way to the hall. She just gave a little smile. I didn't think about this until later.

Starless

No Star at the bus stop today.

Lizzie got on, and we sat in silence for once. This exam thing takes it out of you. Don't know what IT is but I certainly had a lot of it taken.

The Year Seven looked weird sitting in Star's seat. He turned round and stared.

'Where is she?' he asked accusingly. No respect for their elders, these pubescent tweenies.

'I presume you mean, "Where is Amaryllis, please?"' sniffed Lizzie haughtily.

Szechuan red flooded up his neck, over his face and all the way to his hairline so that I felt sorry for him. Lizzie can be a bit scary. Then he scowled. Uh-oh! I saw a little tiny hint of defiance there! His boy hormones must be germinating.

'Amma wot?' he grunted. 'Thought she was called Star!'

'She isn't really,' said Lizzie at the same time as I said, 'She is.'

Long pause while we were all confused.

'Star hasn't got exams today,' I told him. 'Lizzie and I do ICT. Star doesn't. But she'll be in tomorrow. We've got music.'

'Why do you want to know?' asked Lizzie.

He shrugged. 'Just do.'

'Perhaps he fancies older women.' Lizzie's stage whisper is as loud as words through a megaphone. We watched while the crispy backs of his ears burned even redder.

'Perhaps he fancies Boss Woman,' I sniggered.

Then I realised that Boss Woman hadn't been on the bus for a while. I coloured up Szechuan red as I remembered the last time I had seen her. I hope she wasn't avoiding me and my amorous four-legged friend.

Woeful Wednesday

I was only going in for a little bit of my art. No Lizzie, no Star. Boring.

No one to talk to on my bus.

All of a sudden Something Large and Loud *whoomphed* down next to me.

'Don't like to see you all alone, M,' he boomed. 'You miss those girlies, don't you?'

'I can cope on my own, thank you, Jono. In fact, I quite like it. I like the solitude. I like the time to think.'

'Mmmm,' he goes. 'What do you think about? Nail extensions? Noddy Nonchalant?'

That cut me like a sword! Not the Unspeakable's patronising comments, but the thought of the Beautiful Stranger. Woe is me, because I hadn't seen my love for years! And now this scabby Ratcliffe fan, this travesty of a cook, this loud smasher-up of dreams, this – this – *Jono Watkins* – was sullying my Beautiful Stranger by even speaking his name!

All right, not his real name. Even I don't know that. But you know what I mean.

I said (with great dignity), 'I am thinking about my art, Jonathan. It is my very favemost thing.'

'I'm impressed.'

I could feel him peering at me, very near to my face but I wasn't going to meet his eyes. And then he said, 'Course, Emma, I'm artistic. But you can't do everything. My artistic flair comes out in my music and of course in my food preparation. I'm thinking, prepare food and photograph it for magazines. And then eat it.'

'Well, nobody else would want to eat what you'd made!' I said, quick as a flash.

He just laughed. How thick is his skin! Others would be slain by my quick wit, but not him.

He said, 'If I have a summer party, M, maybe you'd like to help me with the catering? Star says you're a good cook. But you've never cooked anything for me.'

Was this 'good cook' bit a compliment? I was cross to feel my face going hot.

I said, 'Maybe I'll do something for your party, Jonathan.

Maybe. But I would be cooking good food, not junk. Crunchy veggies to stick in sophisticated dips. Celery boats full of spicy cream cheese. Real pizza. Maybe fajitas and good salsa. Decent garlic bread. I would be pushing your party food right upmarket.'

Where was all this coming from?

'But I have a very tight summer schedule,' I added, in case he thought his luck was in.

He said, 'Emma, what I would really really like is for you to make me a chocolate cake. I hear your chocolate cake is out of this world. I would buy the ingredients, of course. Lots of chocolate. An' I'd make sure it was fair-trade chocolate, if that's an issue.' He put his head on one side and put on a little boy lost face.

Hmmmmm . . .

He would have to do better than that.

Thinking Thursday

'I called in at the café last night,' cried Lizzie. 'The Patriarch insisted on coming too but I made him wait outside the door. He's so loud. Anyway, I can work every Saturday from the beginning of July! That's what Great Uncle Good Looking said.'

'Suppose I ought to get a summer job,' I said.

'You could do that garden centre job again,' suggested Star.

'No way. I only lasted a week. Utter exploitation! I had

to water things all day long and take off old petals and stagger around with geraniums. But I could certainly use some dosh. I could even buy that black jacket.'

'I've got my Theatre Fortnight to look forward to!' cried Lizzie. 'What are you doing, Star? Wakey Wakey! Are you going on holiday anywhere?

'I don't know,' said Star.

So how was Thursday? On the bus home Lizzie and I decided it was another day of the three Ts – Torture, Testing and Tiredness. You get used to it after a while. You get sort of numbed down. And then at last it was

Freedom Friday!

and that means the day when I might jump off the bus at the Beautiful One, and the day of Alexandra's party, and the day I had to take in a tin full of cookies for us all. Great Huge Cookies! They just spread and spread across the baking tray like crunchy jellyfish. Thirty golden cookies for the form – sorry, thirty-one because of Dodo. Then it all took ages to make because my sisters wailed and wept and sulked and I had to make some for them, too.

I got a smart tin with goats on. I think one of my mother's friends bought it from one of those old stately castles they like to look round and fantasise about. I lined it with kitchen paper, packed in the cookies and rammed on the lid.

Recipe for Great Huge Cookies later if I get the time.

'What's in your tin, M?' cried the Unspeakable the minute I got on the bus. 'Let me see. C'mon, be kind. Soon you won't see me for three whole months.'

'Heaven!' I crowed.

I prised off the lid to let him see them, thinking, their golden aroma will drive him wild all the way through exams.

The top layer flew all over the floor. I grovelled under the seats to rescue them. One GHC had landed in something truly hairy. I picked it up carefully, tucked it down the side and put a bit of kitchen paper over it.

That one had somebody's name on it . . .

When I straightened up at last, Star was in her place in front of me, stashing her stuff under the seat in front. She sat up, neat and serious inside her shell, already for this special day.

Next stop. Lizzie swept down the bus, throwing back her hair and hollering triumphantly, 'The final hour! Party tonight and then all new beginnings! Life is change, petals!'

Dodo Dollop was ecstatic that morning. I suppose he had a few weeks without us to look forward to, but even so he's not usually so over the top. He had another even better new pair of trousers. These were *tailored*. These were *cream*. I mean, none of the boys would have been seen dead in them, but they weren't bad for Dodo-age men, and he had an acceptable navy shirt, too.

He stood up and walked round to the front of his little table and cleared his throat and said, 'I am fully confident that *my* form, my 11D, will shine in the results. Furthermore, I am fully confident I will win the staffroom sweepstake. Thirdly, I am fully confident you will all go on to do whatever it is you want to do, 11D.'

'11D. Always sounds like a bra size to me,' said the Unspeakable.

'Everything sounds like bras to you,' I snapped. 'Sir! I may not go on to whatever it is I want to do, because I don't *know* what it is!'

'Oh. Well, Emma, I am sure your grades will point you in the right direction.'

That sounded like teacher's twaddle to me.

'Mr Donaldson,' said Star, 'May I have a word?'

'Of course, Amaryllis.'

Star had a flush of colour across her face. She cleared her throat and said 'I have looked up blue stocking, Mr Donaldson, and I don't mind you calling me one, because I do love my books. But I must draw your attention to the inherent sexism of your remark. I know on your part it is unthinking, but you don't tease Tunde about all his reading, do you? Or, for that matter, Scott. All right, I don't wear lots of make-up or frills but I keep myself clean and I try to be presentable.'

'And you look terrific, Star!' boomed Jono. 'Looks *and* brains, babe!'

She blushed again. Her chin was tilted up. This was so defiant for Star! This was confidence, or personal growth or something . . . except I saw her lip quiver.

'Star,' I said. 'It's just sir putting his great huge foot in it. You mustn't get upset.'

Dodo was swallowing and looking guilty.

'I'm sorry Star, I really am,' he said, all morose. 'It was p-patronising of me, I suppose. I – I'm having to rethink a lot of things lately.'

He sounded as if he was on one of those TV confessionals . . . *More, Dodo, more! Bring on your murky past, some staffroom scandal, some stock-cupboard groping!*'

'Apology accepted,' said Star graciously. She even managed a small wan smile.

And so, we went all the way through another day all on the edge, pushing our way through the last exams, glancing at our watches, trying to keep the brain cells whizzing, getting a lump in the throat every time we caught sight of someone who wouldn't be there next term, longing for four o'clock and in a funny kind of way dreading it too.

At last it was over!

Pandemonium! Great Huge Cookies and fizzy drinks, cameras out and loud Watkins music!

'Paradise!' screamed Lizzie, throwing herself across a table. 'All I have to think about now is Good Looking the Youngest, and holidays and stage school and –'

'And parties and all day and all night garage sessions with the Devastation,' shouted Jono. '*WOW*! *Will you take a look out there!*'

a vision in powder-blue

'Ooh! That's the car I want!' cried Lizzie. 'Although I think I might have silver.'

'Who cares about the colour, woman!' cried Jono. 'It's a Lotus! Although I think that style is challenged in the testosterone department. I would take a ride in it if the babe was luscious enough, but for myself, I'd want a Lotus Seven.'

'And me!' cried Dean, who always agrees with the Unspeakable.

We gawped at the sports car in the carpark, so pretty and so powder-blue. I'd love to have a convertible like that and brroom! with my hair streaming out . . . although my hair couldn't cope with it and I think Basil might turn wild and feral and jump out, I'd have to strap him in somehow and fix him in a helmet with ear flaps.

'Must be somebody's mum made good' said Dean. 'She's married money, a millionaire. No teacher could afford that car. Big black sunglasses. Look! Dodo has gone over to chat her up.'

Larf! We fell about as we saw Dodo trotting across to the Lotus, all hopeful and smiling.

'Hey, babe, let me drive your car!' drawled Jono in his Dodo Dollop voice. 'Ah'm so cool, Ah'm a Cool Roody Dudey Dodo Dollopalot.'

The driver slid out of the blue Lotus, long legs first with gold sandals and needle heels, and stood up in her cream sundress. She took off her black sunglasses.

'But I know her!' cried Jono.

So did I. I'd know that expensive hair anywhere.
Boss Woman.

Dodo's Perfect Day

'And this is my classroom!' cried Dodo, eyes popping with pride. 'And this band of cheeky individuals is my class!'

'Hello class,' she said. She went all bashful pink.

'11D! This is Miss Grey.' He turned to her and his voice dropped to a whisper as if he knelt before an idol. 'This is Karen.'

Silence. Gobsmack.

It was Jono Watkins who remembered his manners.

He said, 'Good to meet you, Miss Karen. Dodo – er, Mr Donaldson – has been our form teacher for a couple of years now, we are – er – pleased to say . . .'

'Three years!' cried Lizzie, 'and never a day too long!'

'He talks about you all such a lot,' said Boss Woman. She was a little bit *shorter* than me. She said, 'He tells me about all his hopes for you. Don't you, Tim?'

Tim! TIM?

'That's nice,' I stuttered because I had to make a noise of some sort because it had gone all quiet. They were gazing at each other. Rosy cheeks, cow eyes. *Hot Breath, Hammering Heart* . . .

It was LURVE! Everybody was kind of hypnotised. How did our teacher get someone like her? Was there something wrong with her, something we didn't know about?

Ashad hissed, loud enough for the whole of the Albert Hall to hear, 'There must be more to Dodo than meets the eye.'

I thought, *that's* why he's stopped sighing and moping. That's why he dresses coolly now. Boss Woman would never ever tolerate two-in-one trousers with a reinforced seat and storm flaps. She was gazing round our room as if it was the Sistine Chapel.

'Sir's brightened it up a bit recently,' said Lizzie accusingly. 'We used to have tatty brown notice-boards. All holes and old Blu-Tak and bits of Sellotape. None of these plants or nice posters. Are you giving Mr Donaldson a lift home in your Lotus?'

'You'll need a bike rack,' said Jono.

'No bike today because we are off on an adventure,' she said.

The words, 'adventure' and 'Dodo' just don't go together. I pictured him boinging head first off a bridge on a big elastic band, spinning in churny white water like a teddy in a washing machine, or sliding painfully down a rock. Yet I heard myself say,

'Sir can cope with anything.'

Boss Woman turned to me and glowed and I knew she loved to hear that.

A gleam of recognition flickered in her eyes. She said, 'Haven't I seen you on the bus? And – you have a little dog, don't you? How is he? Still lively?'

'He's – er – fine. But why haven't you got that big ring any more?'

Who said that? What a nosy heffa!

'Anyone can make a mistake,' she whispered. 'I met your wonderful teacher, just in time!'

We had common ground between us, I thought, Basil and Dodo.

'Did you give the ring back?' I whispered. I can't help being interested, you see.

'Yes.'

'But not the car?'

'The car is mine,' said Boss Woman firmly. 'I *earned* the car.'

The spell of Dodo's secret love was broken because the felt pens were out. We were signing shirts. It is an important Year Eleven ritual, a bonding, you see. I felt someone writing on my back and then a Voice murmured, 'Oh my god, M. You are so very, very nosy! How can you ask such personal stuff? You have only just met her.'

'I am interested in my fellow human beings, Jono,' I explained. 'I am a naturally curious girl. And, actually, we have had a previous encounter.' I really wanted to know how she earned that car, but I didn't quite have the nerve to ask. Not that time, anyway.

'You sound like a tabloid hack, M,' he said.

Now there's a thought, Jono . . . but what are you

writing on my back? It's taking a very long time.

I watched Boss Woman Karen's eyes seek Dodo Dollop as if he was the only thing in the whole world that mattered. Guess what! I blinked back some soppy tears!

You see, Dodo wasn't bad. He cared about us in his own way, and he was my form teacher *and only for a few more seconds!*

I grabbed my tin of Great Huge Cookies and held them out.

Boss Woman cooed, 'How delicious.' She took a cookie and broke it in half – a piece for her and one for Dodo. 'This will set us up for our adventure.'

'Er, excuse me, what kind of adventure would this be?' Would you believe the Unspeakable? He had just accused me of being nosy!

'Actually, it's a murder weekend,' said Boss Woman. 'We're off to a spooky castle in Northumberland. Murder and a four-course dinner. Murder most foul, and out damned spot.'

'I know that one!' cried Jono. 'It's Lady Macbeth. Innit, Star. Star?'

Boss Woman took Dodo's hand. 'Show me your school, please, Tim,' she said and meek and mild second-in-command Timothy Dodo led her away. It was his Perfect Day.

'Life is full of surprises, innit?' said Jono, all unspeakably philosophical. 'If Dodo has found his soul mate there's hope for us all.'

'Not for all of us,' said Cath Ratcliffe in her dark snaky way. Funny how she can always make things sound horrible.

'Ah! Cath. You missed out on the cookies,' I smiled. 'Excuse fingers.'

'Thanks, Emma,' she said as she took a big bite of the one I had reserved especially for her.

'Mmmm, have they got golden syrup in them? They're really gooey and sticky, mmmm.'

I noticed that the Spot Fairy had visited Cath Ratcliffe. Bigtime.

Let's hear it for the Spot Fairy!

little marble made of ice

'Hey, there's Star's chocolates too,' cried Luke.

'Don't you think you should let her pass them round, Mr Manners?' I said.

'Yeah, OK. But where is she?'

'She's around somewhere,' said Lizzie.

'Yeah,' said Jono, 'she's going home with you lot tonight, isn't she?'

'Oh?' I said. 'We hadn't sorted anything. I thought we'd meet later at Alexandra's.'

All I could think about, (*Hot Breath, Hammering Heart*) was, dare I ask the Beautiful Stranger to the party? Will I see him again this Friday?

The Unspeakable helped himself to another cookie. I

grabbed his hand to get it back and the cookie got crushed and broken.

'Now look what you've done!' I shrieked. 'That's not your cookie and now it's crumbled.'

'It's in its contract,' he said. He is so . . . *Unspeakable*.

He said, 'Well, Star told me she was going back with you. And she had lots of bags of stuff.'

She did, didn't she . . .

There was a little cold spot in my middle. It was like a marble. It was made of ice and it was getting bigger as if it was rolling around in the snow. I thought, why didn't Star arrange to go to the party with Lizzie or me? I remembered her now at Jono's party, telling me that it was the only one she had been to because she wouldn't go on her own. Why didn't I think to ask her to come with me?

I stared at the box of chocolates. There was a tag on them, a pretty shiny blue tag. I turned it over. Inside, in Star's handwriting, it said:

> *To all my dear friends and Mr Dollop.*
> *Good luck and have a lovely summer.*

They were the finest Belgian chocolates, plain and milk and white, it said. Expensive. Special.

'Were you two talking about Brain Girl?' called Cath Ratcliffe, pushing past me towards the chocolates, 'Because she left ages ago.'

They were Goodbye Chocolates.

Run, Star, run

She left ages ago . . .

Lizzie and I looked at each other.

Lizzie said, 'I've got a bad, bad feeling.'

I ran for the door. Lizzie shouted, 'What about Alexandra's party?'

I turned back, grabbed my bag and ran again.

I knew they were coming after me, those great huge Unspeakable feet, pounding down the corridor and outside. I skirted round the crowds, the Unspeakable charged straight through the middle. I stopped at the school gates, gasping for air. My heart was thudding somewhere near my ears, not nice, I looked up the road, and down and all around.

No Star. No Star in sight.

Jono skidded to a halt by me, and cried, 'Why the panic, M? What is it?'

'HOW CAN YOU BE SO STUPID, JONO!'

It came out all of a rush. 'She's not been happy. And I knew! I should have done something!'

Lizzie rushed up and doubled over, wheezing. I was just beginning to put it all together. I saw in my mind's eye Star's puffy eyes. I could hear her silence.

Jono peered right into my face. 'You mean you've not talked to her about it?' he growled. 'Star has seemed kinda . . . little, lately.'

'Shut up, Jono. Don't be so accusing!' I yelled. 'I suppose you know exactly how your friends feel about every little thing?'

'That's different,' he said. 'We're guys.'

'That's junk, Jono, that's sexist junk!' I shouted, and I could feel the tears brimming.

He said, 'But you three have always been so close. Such good friends! And Star's got a lot of baggage to handle, hasn't she?'

Silence. I felt awful. Judging by Lizzie's face, she did too.

'She ran for the bus,' said a voice down by my side. 'She ran ever so fast. She's got very long legs, hasn't she?'

It was Tuba Boy, looking up into my face. He said again, 'Star. The one you call Amaryllis. She ran after a bus.'

Oh! the relief! Lizzie grabbed my arm and hung there, going, 'Thank god! Thank god!'

'No, not our proper bus home,' said Tuba Boy. 'She got a bus that goes the other way.'

spread your wings and fly

'Send for Dodo!' yelled Lizzie.

'No, Lizzie! What could he do? He'd just phone Star's dad and I'm beginning to think that's a great huge pot of trouble . . . Anyway, he's gone off with BW.'

'Who's BW?'

'Shut up, Jono, and let me think . . . where could she have gone?'

We stood there, the three of us, and Tuba Boy. Scared stiff.

Then Jono said, 'Hey. I bet she's gone to France. That's where her mum is, isn't it?'

'But it's the party,' cried Lizzie. 'Surely she wouldn't want to miss that? But then I guess she's not a party animal, is she?'

'What'll we do, what'll we ever do?' I wailed, and the tears burst out all hot. I felt real, real panic. 'Star can't possibly survive Paris! Star even gets lost in the shopping centre! She's so trusting. They'll see her coming!'

'Who will? The French aren't that bad.'

'I don't mean the French, Jono, I mean every nasty person anywhere! Star's so daffy in her real life. I know she's dead clever in school, but she's got no common sense at all!'

The ice marble had grown and flooded over the whole of my insides.

'It's all right, Emma,' said Jono. 'Just calm down, we can sort it.'

But in my head someone screamed, *PANIC! PANIC ATTACK FOR ABSOLUTE REAL!*

I don't ever ever want children. It's bad enough having to worry about your friends.

'Star can't have gone far. She's got no money,' he said.

'Yes she has! She gets money from the old ladies' tea

rooms. She says they insist on leaving little tips. Alfred, and Mrs Blake and Violet . . . she hardly ever goes out, except with us. She could have saved up a fortune.'

'Emma! Keep things in proportion. Calm down,' he said, trying to be all masterful, but I saw his eyes flicker and *they* weren't calm. He was worried too.

One-way ticket

the wrong bus

I didn't want to think of Star on a strange bus. Not a bus that was taking her away from Lizzie and Jono and me.

It's something to do with feeling left out, excluded, wasn't it?

I remember her at Jono's party. She said her dad didn't have time for her any more.

Why didn't I realise how unhappy she was?

Now she was leaving.

On the wrong bus. And probably with a single ticket. No return.

girls' thing

'No, Jono you can't come!' There was a big crowd of us at the gates now, all Jono's lot, all frowning and shifting from foot to foot, worrying.

'But I know my way around the airport, M!' he insisted.

'Back off, Jono. This is a girls' thing,' said Lizzie firmly. 'I don't think Star would want you to be there. But you could take our bags home with you, we won't want to carry them all that way.' She dropped her bag at Ashad's feet and I plonked mine before Jono – I couldn't carry cookie tins to the airport! Jono grabbed my hand and started writing on the back. I tried to snatch it away and he cried, 'It's my mobile, Stupid! You might just need my help!'

'Fat chance. But you can lend us some money for a taxi,' I said.

'Oh all right,' he said, emptying his pockets. 'Ashad? Tunde?' he called. 'Got any spare dosh?'

We did well there. As it turned out, we had enough money for a taxi all the way to the airport.

Question A – have you ever tried to get a taxi at half past four on a Friday afternoon?

In the end we had to send the Unspeakable off down to the main road to get one and bring it back to school for us.

'See you later at the party?' he called out as we were whizzed away in the taxi with Lizzie screeching, 'Follow that plane!'

It took ages to get to East Midlands Airport. The traffic was terrible. Friday traffic, I suppose.

Question B – Have you ever tried to find someone in an airport when they weren't looking for you? There are so many people at airports. None of them look normal. None of them were Star. There were hundreds of families with little kids screaming for things from the shops and old couples shuffling off to the Canary Islands in beige leisure shoes and parsnip slacks with elasticated waists.

'How do we find her? I bet she's changed her clothes,' wailed Lizzie. 'If she was still in her uniform, she'd stand out in the crowd, like they always want us to on school trips.'

'Let's check out the planes on the board,' I said. 'Then we can narrow it down to concourse.'

'What?' said Lizzie with her face all screwed up. 'You do show off, M. M for Big Mouth!'

'Stop it Lizzie! The stress is turning you into a witch! Now, where would she fly to? She has told me where her mum works, but I can't remember the name of the town.'

'Great!' sneered Lizzie. She put on a really bimbo voice and wittered, 'Excuse me, what time is the plane to somewhere in France with a college?'

I squeezed my eyes tight shut. Brain cells and motor neurones, and sparky bits, get transmitting those little signals, *get working, and join up why don't you*!

'It's near Paris,' I said. 'Her mum works in a college in a town near Paris, but I can't remember the name. Lizzie, what can we do?'

'Maybe she'd have to get a plane to Paris to start with?'

We ran across the airport and stood craning our necks to see one of those little telly things.

There were no planes to Paris on it.

'Then she isn't getting one,' moped Lizzie.

'Don't give up yet,' I cried.

I hurried to the timetable board. There had been a flight to Paris, at ten past four! It arrived in Paris at twenty past five. I screamed 'Oh no! She's up there! Star is up there, all on her own!'

'No she's not. She's up in a plane with a pilot and some nice stewards.'

'But listen, Lizzie, she's never flown before, she's unhappy, she'll get lost, be sick, and be terrified and bombed by terrorists, abducted and –'

'*HELP!*' screamed Lizzie. '*HELP! ABDUCTION! BOMBS! KIDNAP! RAPE!*'

For a second I couldn't decide if it was Actress Lizzie or Real Lizzie throwing a wobbly. It worked. A policeman in a stiff waistcoat hurried across. He had a gun on his belt – or was it his mobile phone, I don't know, but he looked serious.

'What's the matter, young ladies?' he asked. 'Have you found a suspicious package?'

'No, it's our friend, Star – Amaryllis. Our friend! She's run away!' I cried. 'And she's no good at that kind of thing.'

'Where is she, where is she?' sobbed Lizzie.

And then I noticed them for the first time.

Rows of glossy magazines. And beyond them?

Books.

'C'mon!' I shouted, dashing towards the books, with

Lizzie panting behind me, dodging pushchairs and clumps of people with golf clubs and through the racks of magazine, past the fat books with shiny gold writing. I crashed into a man in an emerald green donkey's sombrero and an orange tan and he said something ever so rude, but I knew if Star was in this airport, which she must be because she was still at school when the plane left for Paris, it would be by the books.

Lizzie saw her first.

Star was kneeling in the corner, head down, reading.

We sat down either side of her.

I said, 'Time to come home, Star.'

She jumped and turned to me, and then her face softened into a great huge smile.

She said obediently, 'Yes, of course, M. This book isn't very good anyway. The writing is poor.'

And she put it back on the shelf and stood up. Her face was all crumpled.

'Star, just what are you doing?' I said, trying to stop my voice from wobbling. She would cry if I wasn't careful.

'I wanted to get on a plane,' she said, 'but they wouldn't sell me a ticket. I didn't know you had to book so far ahead. They wouldn't let me go. I didn't know what to do next, and then I saw some books . . .'

'Listen to me, you two,' shouted Lizzie 'I am in severe stress and shock and starvation. I need chips. Now!'

'Lizzie, it's an airport, the food will be expensive and not very nice.'

'We've got the Wot Kin's money,' she insisted, 'and they'd want us to spend it, they'd want to be part of the Rescuing Star operation. They wouldn't want us to feel hungry and weak.'

'I have money too,' said Star. 'Enough for blueberry muffins if you like.'

So it was chips and vinegar and blobs of red ketchup and cola and muffins amongst screaming kids and their cross parents. Lizzie waved across at the policeman. 'Crisis over!' she cooed.

There was even enough for a taxi home. And in the taxi I sent the Unspeakable a text message saying, Star is safe with us now.

We were too late and too tired to go to the pool party, it would be over by now, so it was back to my house for

---

ELEVEN O'CLOCK CHOCOLATE CAKE

You will need:
- 110g self-raising flour
- 110g sugar (not the healthy kind)
- 110g marg or butter
- bit of baking powder
- 2 large or 3 medium really free-range eggs because you don't want to think of chicky-chucks all squashed together thousands to a barn, all squabbling and depressed, and then the farmer shouting PUSH! YOU LOT!

1. Sift flour, baking powder and cocoa into a bowl and chuck in the rest. Except the

chocolate.

2. Get some whizzers and whizz it all up.

3. Wipe butter round the inside of a tin. My mother recommends a tin with a loose bottom(!!!)

4. Dollop in the mixed-up stuff

5. Give Star and Lizzie each a whizzer to lick and then clean out your bowl yourself with as many fingers of both hands as you can get in.

6. Bake it at 3/170°C for about half an hour. Get your oven gloves on when doing anything hot!

While it's baking melt the chocolate in a bowl hot water. Then when it's a bit cool, dribble lots of gooey melted cloc all over! Lick bowl and fingers.

Oh. And heat the oven up properly first or else it doesn't work.

While you are waiting for it to cook, talk to your very best friends of all and be thankful that you can.

Don't go down that road

'I just can't seem to get on with Lynn,' Star said. 'The first time we met and Dad said, "Lynn I would like you to meet Amaryllis," she just stood and stared at me. I could smell her perfume. It was . . . sharp. I smiled and I took a step forward but then I stopped. She didn't smile back. She has never touched me. She puts up a shield.'

'What about her kids?' I asked.

'We're just so different from each other. They call me Swot and Know-all. They say I show off when I read my books. And they say, "Why haven't you got a boyfriend? Kate has, and she's younger than you." They say it all in whispers.'

'Doesn't your dad defend you?'

'I don't think he notices,' she said. Generously, I thought. She went on, 'He just feels awkward. He clears his throat all the time as if he's got a daddy long-legs in there. He says he didn't realise how *unnatural* it was.'

'How unnatural what was?'

Star looked very small that night. She's not really. She's taller than I am.

'He means *me*. He says he didn't understand how hard it would be to have me in a white family.'

'What is he talking about?' cried Lizzie. 'He should be proud of a daughter like you, all clever and kind! I mean, look at my family, we are lots of different shades and hair bits. I'm more like George the Patriarch and Michael is like Mum. We're all bits and pieces, everyone is, unless they live in a little tiny hamlet cut off from the rest of the world and then you get . . .'

'Thanks, Lizzie, don't let's go down that road,' I said.

'My dad didn't mean to be unkind to me,' said Star

defensively. 'He just doesn't know what to do, I can tell. He's trying to please everyone. And there are three of them. I just don't fit in.'

I said, 'Doesn't sound as if they try to fit in with you! Star, why couldn't you tell us about it, really tell us?'

'You might have thought they were right,' she said. 'You might have joined in. You might have shunned me too.'

'Star, you're our friend!' shrieked Lizzie. 'We don't do shunning!'

Star said, 'I keep thinking about that poem, "They flee from me, that sometime did me seek". I mean, I know it is not about dads, but that's how I feel. Forsaken. You know that poem?'

Lizzie and I looked at each other. Lizzie said, 'Can't recall it just now.'

I said, 'Star, do you tell your mum you are unhappy? You write to her, don't you?'

She hung her head and said in a small voice, 'No. I mean, yes I write, every fortnight, but I don't tell her all about my feelings. It wouldn't be fair. I should cope. You see Mum is a loner. She told me she was never meant to be in a couple or a family. She's tried and it didn't work, but she thought I should be in a family, while she went to France. Mum and Dad thought they were doing the fair thing, but it's turned out bad. I don't work in a family. I should be on my own too.'

'No *you* are supposed to be with other people! You can't just think you're the same as your mum. Nothing stays the same. Things change, all the time. And what would Lizzie and I do without you?' Star burst into tears. Lizzie was next, loud and thorough sobbing, and then me. I couldn't bear to think of unhappy Star, all by herself, worrying. I wrapped my arms round her and Lizzie tried to cuddle both of us. Basil saw his chance and joined in the hug.

Time for chocolate cake, even if it's ready long before eleven o'clock. Time to watch that melted chocolate trickling across the top and over the edge and down the sides, so dark and shiny.

You can double the amount and make a humungous great huge cake, or two reasonable cakes. I made an extra little one for Sophie and Sarah and left it for them to eat in the morning. 11 o'Clock Chocolate Cake is at its very best still a bit warm in a bowl with a spoon.

You can splodge on ice cream if you like, or plain yoghurt, or cream if you're feeling truly greedy.

You can melt up a truly gooey middle layer for it, spreading on a tin of that thick sweet condensed milk mixed with more chocolate.

You can sprinkle it with little silver cake balls, or chocolate sprinkles.

You can whoosh it around with a fork.

You can wedge in bits of chocolate flake.

There are many ways of eating 11 o'Clock Chocolate Cake. Whichever way you choose to eat it, you'll feel better.

Unless you eat far too much. Then that's your fault.

I'm only sixteen. So many ways to eat chocolate cake. So many things to look forward to in life. But I still can't make out what the Unspeakable has written on the back of my school shirt because it has smudged in the Star crisis . . . something about Emma . . . M . . . Mine . . . something with 'ake' in it too . . .

fluffy lizard

'I don't think I could eat any more,' said Star, putting down her bowl by her sleeping bag.

'We'll need some for the morning anyway,' I said.

'It *is* the morning,' she said. 'We're eating 11 o'Clock Cake at half past one.'

Her face was blotchy. Her eyes were swollen. They looked like pink sugared almonds, but she was better for the crying, sort of soft and open now, and Basil had helped by trying to clean her up. I suppose he liked the mix of salty tears and chocolate.

'Basil,' she said, stroking his ears, 'you're like a fluffy lizard.'

We were too tired to think about going to sleep. And something was pushing me on to sort Star although part of me didn't want to. It was like waiting at the exam hall door again, wanting to get in there and face all those questions you had dreaded, but wanting to run away to the ice-cream park instead.

I wiped my finger round the bowl for the very last of

the chocolate, and said, 'So, Star, I suppose you told your dad and Lynn you were staying here?'

'Yes. I suppose I sort of lied to them.'

'I suppose you sort of did,' said Lizzie.

I sucked my finger till it tasted of finger. 'How long did you tell them you were staying?'

'I said I was staying for the weekend. I didn't think past that. Just long enough to escape.'

'So they won't worry until Sunday night?'

She hunched her shoulders and the tears welled up again. 'I don't know – if – if they'll worry at all,' she whispered.

'Of course they will, at least your dad will. All parents worry,' I said.

Aagh! Was I sounding like my own mother?

'I think we must tell your mum, Star.'

Lizzie said, ever tactful, 'I'd be furious with my parents if they did that to me!'

'What else could they do?' cried Star at the same time as I was shouting, 'Shut up Lizzie!'

Star swallowed hard. She said, 'All right. I suppose I am angry. I would like to live with both of them. That is not to be. But if I tell Mum she'll be upset! I don't want her to think I can't cope. And you see I didn't even know you had to book planes and the woman at the airport said there weren't any flights to – to where I wanted to go.'

'There were flights to Paris,' I said, puzzled. 'And your

mum will want to know if you're unhappy. She'll want to help. She's your mum. It's in her contract to worry about your happiness. Have you got a number for her in France? Star? STAR!'

She was head down, not looking at me, stroking Basil and humming to herself. She was like Sarah and Sophie when they want to pretend they can't see me.

'Star! You have got a number for her, haven't you? Give it here.'

Lizzie said, 'M for meddling!' but Star fumbled in her bag for a notebook and handed it to me.

She said, 'I've never used the number. Lynn complains about the phone bill. So I don't know if that's the right bit for France at the front. And M, you've got a chocolate moustache.'

'We can soon check the code,' I said, wiping my face with Basil's tail. 'Come on.'

I felt so efficient as we hurtled downstairs. I could solve all this, it was only numbers. We checked the code.

'You dial, M,' said Star.

'It's late at night,' said Lizzie.

'This is an emergency,' I told her.

We stood in the hall, listening to the *brrr* of the French phone, all those hundreds of miles away. Nothing. Nobody picked it up and suddenly I knew why.

'Star, they won't be at the college now! They're probably only a couple of hours before or after us, and they won't be at work now.'

'Of course! They'll all be out eating snails and garlic!' cried Lizzie.

'No,' said Star. 'That's not the college, that's the number of her flat.'

'Maybe I did it wrong. There are an awful lot of numbers.' I tried again. No result.

'We'd better write a letter,' announced Lizzie. 'You can write it, Star, but we'll supervise. I don't think you're saying the right things. Something like, "Dear Mum, lovely weather here, but Mum come and get me because I can't stand it because they leave me out of everything and they are so BLOODY HORRIBLE –"'

'Sssh! Shut up Lizzie!' Too late. I heard a door open upstairs.

'What on earth are you lot doing?' hissed my mum. 'You'll wake Sarah and Sophie. You've already woken Dad and me.'

'Erm – I'll pay you some money towards the call,' I mumbled.

'Why? Where are you phoning?'

'France.'

'WHAT?'

'I'm sorry, Mrs Peek, it's my fault,' said Star. 'My mum works in France, you see . . .'

My mother blinked. I could almost hear her brain ticking.

She said, 'You just phone away, Star.' And she went back upstairs.

We did. We counted to fifty while the phone rang. No one answered.

Basil cleans up

I should have known, because Basil usually follows me everywhere, especially when my friends are round.

He hadn't come downstairs with us. I didn't think about that until I went back into the bedroom and *caught him in the act*.

'Basil!' I screeched but he licked even faster in case I beat him to the very last smear.

'Oh well, we'd eaten most of it anyway,' said Star.

'He's cleaned the bowls nicely,' said Lizzie. 'He could get a job at the Good Looking Café doing dishes.'

'We'll try again in the morning, Star,' I said. 'I'll even talk to the parents if that's OK by you. They might know a way of contacting her.'

'I'm still not sure it's the best thing to do . . .'

'You must think positively, Star!' announced Lizzie. 'You're fantastic. Loads of people think so! You've got us, and Jono and Ashad and Dean and Adam and Tunde and even Dodo! You'll go off to uni in a couple of years and if you don't sort something in the meantime, I bet you could live with M and me.'

'Thanks, Lizzie,' said Star, 'but maybe you should check with your parents first.'

'They'll agree,' announced Lizzie. 'Michael will be away

from home in September so you could have his room. My mum likes you and the Patriarch will do what he's told. You see, all these people love you to bits. Think of your old folks at the tea rooms. Think of Tuba Boy!'

Love letters straight from somebody or other's heart

Star clapped her hand to her mouth.

'Lizzie! You've just reminded me. Tuba Boy. He gave me a letter outside school tonight but I didn't have time to open it because I was running away. Maybe it's about more books.'

She got up and delved into the side pockets of her bag. She brought out a crumpled envelope and began ironing it with the back of her hands.

'Never mind smoothing, woman!' cried Lizzie. 'Look at the handwriting! That's never been written by Tuba Boy. Get it open at once!'

She went to snatch it from Star who held it close and said firmly, 'No. This is mine. Do you know, this must have been a really smart envelope before Tuba Boy got hold of it.'

'Get it open, Star! The suspense is killing me,' I cried. I would have ripped open such a letter, if I'd ever got one. Star had to take the ex-chocolate cake knife to it.

And do you know what? *She went to wash it in the bathroom first!*

Dear Star

What a gr8 name. I've never heard it before but my little brother Sam says that is what U R called. He made a bit of a mistake and earwigged on your friend's e-mail address. She's very nice, but it's U I've been looking out 4. I'm sometimes at the bus stop on my way to college. Saturdays at the moment I'm in the sports shop but I'm finishing there soon. I've got a holiday job every morning in the bookshop round the corner. That's more me.

Sam says U R always reading. Who do U like?

I think U R very pretty.

And U R kind. That's what Sam says.

Craig

'This Craig is putting himself about a bit,' said Lizzie.

'Oh, M, I'm sorry he wasn't your Beautiful Stranger after all,' said Star.

'That's fine!' I said. I realised that I hadn't thought of the Beautiful Stranger for hours and hours. I said, 'Craig must have been a bit amazed when I turned up in the sports shop. As far as I can remember, he was fairly fit. And now I realise he's been at the stop with TB sometimes. He's tall, and dark. Sounds like he'd suit you, Star.'

Her brow puckered. She said, 'I don't really like his style. I mean, using U and R and 8 instead of real words.'

Lizzie snorted with laughter and I said, 'Star! Don't be so picky! That's only cos he does a lot of e-mailing.'

Now Lizzie was doing her Madame Machiavelli number. 'You'll have to meet him, Star. You'll have to go to the shop next week.' Her eyes glinted as she schemed away. 'We could take you there. We could wait for you, and then all go on for lemon cakes.'

'Lizzie. I don't know about that, I –'

'D' you know,' cried Lizzie, 'I think I might be an agony aunt instead of an actress. I am good at sorting people's problems. Agony aunts get to sit on sofas on morning telly, don't they?'

getting to the bottom of the problem under a great huge moon

I lay there thinking, I'd better open more windows – lots of chocolate cake, Basil's bottom . . . Basil was still curled up round Star's feet, so I took him downstairs and let him out into the garden. After all, Saturday morning was Dad's weekly date with the poop scoop. He had to have something useful to do with his life, a purpose.

A great huge yellow moon sat in the sky. I wonder what it looks like from France. Star might have been there! Think of all those men with their wine and their baguettes, shouting *merde* at anybody English. Think of Star all by herself with her big scared eyes.

Think of that great huge moon, shining down on all of us, when our lives were changing. The moon shone on Pram Gran, and Dodo and Karen Grey, Basil and even the

Wot Kin. If the parents weren't so mean and repressive, the moon could have been shining on us girls in Ibiza! We'd wanted to go there after exams, it would be terrific, we'd be so cool and glam with showers and sangria and all night dancing but all the parents could do was witter on about How They Trust Us OF COURSE but not the Others Lurking Behind the Sunbeds who might Just Happen to be Murderers, Robbers and Rapists. So neurotic, these parents!

I'm really glad Star didn't go off far away. She might get ill and not eat and get slipped some bad tablet and have sunstroke and stand on sea-urchins and get stung by jellyfish or be carried away by bandits on bicycles to their mountain lair and ravished and ransomed.

Basil trotted upstairs after me and threw himself back on Star's feet with a deep sigh of contentment. I think I'd rather come back as a small dog than a rabbit.

I lay awake for a while, gazing into the moonlight that slanted between my curtains.

School so far away now . . . everyone going different ways . . . e-mail for Star's mum . . . unless she's a technophobe like Star . . . what are we going to do about Star? She can't go on as she is . . .

white church, purple flowers and little blue fishes

It was still dark when I drifted awake.

That was because the curtains were closed, and there was no moonlight sneaking in.

It was midday.

I could hear Lizzie snuffling and giving little snores. Lizzie talks in her sleep, it's dead funny! Sometimes she sits bolt upright and shouts, 'Wadderyawoodle? Gimmeyat! Nah!' and then falls back down again.

'Star,' I whispered loudly enough to wake her if she wasn't, 'are you awake?'

'Yes,' she said, 'and I'm glad I'm here with you and Lizzie. I think I would be a bit frightened waking up by myself. All alone, on a quay by the sea. Now, there's a poem beginning in my mind, all about the boats and the seawater slapping against the quay . . .'

I thought, I know I did not do geography, but Paris isn't by the sea, is it?

I said, 'Why would you be on a quay by the sea, Star?'

'I thought I'd get ferries between the islands, you see. You have to wait for them, early in the mornings. Maybe wait for them to do their fishing first.'

'Are there many islands in the middle of France?'

'Oh, not France, M. I was going to Greece. To sail the Aegean Sea.'

'By yourself ?'

'No, with the ferryman, or the fisherman. He would be driving the little boat.'

'Star . . . what's this about Greece anyway? We thought you were trying to get a plane to Paris. Blimey, Star!'

'I just wanted to sit and dream among the islands. The islands in the Aegean Sea. How I love those words! I can hear the waves in them, surging on to the rocks then falling away again. The wine-dark sea . . .' She sounded as if she was casting a spell.

She went on, as if I wasn't there, 'I never understood why Homer said it was wine-dark. Maybe the sea is dark as red wine at night? Maybe Homer had different wine. I just wanted to flee away, M. I kept thinking of little white churches with purple flowers. Royal purple flowers, spilling everywhere. Blue, blue sea full of little fishes.'

'And hot sun. And drop-dead gorgeous bronzed boy gods walking the earth. Mmmm. With curly black hair and big chunky monkey arms . . .'

'Well, good morning, Lizzie!'

'Those deep purple flowers are threaded into my hair. I'm sipping coffee, gazing out over a moonlit sea. Music in the clubs thudding away till five o'clock . . .' Lizzie sat bolt upright in her sleeping bag and shouted, 'We won't always be sixteen and poor! Let's go for it, girls! Coming to your little island one summer soon, Lizzie, M and Star! So look out, why don't you!'

There was tapping on the bedroom door.

'They only want to know if there's any of our chocolate cake left,' I groaned. '*Go away Sarah and/or Sophie!*'

'Emma. Star. Wake up!' It was my dad. 'Someone is here.'

someone is here

Someone is here! Who? Probably Jono Watkins knocking

on the door to tell us he's having another skanky party with stale peanuts and too much volume.

'Who is it?'

I thought, please don't let it be Star's dad and Lynn. Things will get said. The whole situation will get burst open like a rotten peach and I'm not sure we can cope with it before breakfast.

'Emma, come on! Just get up and get downstairs. All of you.'

It didn't sound good.

We hopped downstairs. I wore my duvet, Star and Lizzie were in sleeping bags.

My mother was waiting in the hall. She looked kinda excited and clumsy. She glanced at the sleeping bags, but we always wear them the morning after a sleepover. It's traditional.

She said, 'Someone in the sitting room to see you, Star.'

Oh no. Well, we weren't leaving Star on her own to sort it! We were one each side as we shuffled to the doorway but we couldn't get through all at once. We were just a bit jammed.

But there in the sitting room stood a very tall Star.

Star froze for the splitness of a second.

Then she hopped right into her mother's arms.

'Lizzie. Emma. Come on and have some breakfast,' said my mum, pushing us into the kitchen. She fished about in the freezer and found some chocolate croissants. We only have them on special days, like birthdays. She shook out coffee beans into the grinder. Lizzie and I sat at the table and waited. I smelled ground coffee and croissants warming in the oven so that the dark chocolate melted into the crispy layers, and I thought, this is a day when things change.

things change and croissants crisp

When Star and her mum finally came into the kitchen, my mother sat them down at the table. Sophie and Sarah were hovering in the doorway.

Star's mum said, 'It's good to find you in such a warm household, Amaryllis. Your poor father had such a shock when he opened the door to me. He said you often come round here at weekends. I'm pleased you've still got good friends.' She turned to my mother and said, 'Thank you for welcoming Amaryllis into your home, Mrs Peek.'

'It's a pleasure, er, er . . .'

'Natalie. And I'm Natalie King now I'm single again.'

'You should have let me know you were coming, Mum,' cried Star. 'I might have been out! In fact, I was out!'

'I'm sorry, darling. It was a spur of the moment thing. You just . . . your letters gave you away.'

Star frowned. 'But I took ages writing them.'

Her mum took her hand. She said, 'That's just it. Your letters sounded wrong. I knew you were trying to hide some feelings. The words were just too bright. So I phoned the airport and got straight on a plane.'

'How did you do that?' shrieked Star. 'They wouldn't give *me* a ticket straight away!'

Oops . . .

Her mother stared at her. How would Star get out of this one? She wouldn't, not for long. If Star ever gets to the point of speaking, then she has to tell the truth. It's when she doesn't say anything that you should worry.

Her mother said, 'Is everything all right at school?'

'Yes, we've done our exams now. We've got time off.'

'Oh. I see,' said her mother. 'So you can spend time at home with your dad and, er, Lynn and her kids?'

Star looked down and picked up a crumb or two from the table.

The doorbell rang, three piercing bursts.

My dad went to the door, which could have been truly embarrassing because he was decorating in his old saggy jeans with workman's bottom cleavage, but it didn't matter because this time our visitor really was the Unspeakable.

I've never ever seen anyone barge quite like Jono Watkins.

'Ah! So *that's* why you were running, Star. To meet your mum! Hi, Mrs –'

'Natalie. Natalie King.'

'Hi!' grabbing her hand and almost shaking her arm out of its socket. 'Jonathan Watkins. Hi – Hi Mr and Mrs Peek. Basil! How ya doin', mate? Y'know the last time I saw these two,' he was leering at Lizzie and me, 'they were chasing Star to the airport as if all the hounds in hell were after them!'

A short silence.

Lizzie said, her voice sharp as a Texan's steak knife, 'Have you come hoping for your money, Jonathan? Because if so, I am afraid it went on chips.'

'Lizzie, I didn't come for money. Thank you for the text message, M, the laddos and I were all worried sick! We were chuffed that you'd found Star and that you were all right and that Star wasn't on a plane to Africa by mistake, and now I've just come to check on you girlies and – OW! Lizzie, waddyer doin' yer violent woman?'

Star's mum was staring at her, horrified, coffee cup halfway to her lips, but Star cried, 'It's all right, Mum, I had realised I couldn't do it after all!'

'Do what?'

'Couldn't go away on my own. I was just coming back when M and Lizzie found me. I had begun to feel frightened, you see. Well. I was just having a quick look in the bookstall.'

Star began to cry. So did her mum.

Sarah and Sophie stood watching with big eyes, then Sophie started too, and so Lizzie joined in really loudly, and well, I wept too. Something awful might have happened, but instead things had been made better. Not that they were all finished, but still much better. I had a little giggle in the middle of the crying. Relief, I suppose.

'Jonathan. Have a chocolate croissant,' said my mother, blinking hard.

'Oh. Cheers, Mrs Peek,' he said, sitting down, so polite

and quietly spoken, every mother's sweet dream, I don't think so. Jono Watkins, how dare you, getting your feet under my table and your teeth into my chocolate croissants . . . and *my dog on your knee!*

reality and dream

My mother had to grind more coffee beans and scrabble in the freezer for more croissants because my father thought he'd missed out, and, hey! we didn't mind having more.

When everyone had stopped sniffling and was getting on with serious eating, flakes of croissant raining down towards happy Basil, Lizzie said, 'You're such a big mouth, Jono. Your mouth is even bigger than M's.'

'Yeah, soz, Lizzie, I was worrying about Star going to France on her own.'

'She wasn't even going to France, she was off to Greece!' said Lizzie in her 'I told you so' voice. 'She was going to sit by the Aegean Sea.'

'Now who's a big mouth, Lizzie!' I said.

Star's face had gone dark apricot jam colour. She turned up her face to her mum and said, 'That is the truth, Mum. I want to go to Greece. You see, I read some beautiful words by someone called Kazantzakis. I'll get it!' She ran upstairs and ran back down with a scrap of paper. She smoothed it out and read, 'Happy is the man, I thought, who, before dying, has the good fortune to sail the Aegean Sea . . . Nowhere else can one pass so easily and serenely from reality to dream.'

She smiled at her mum. Her mum smiled back. She understood Star, I could see that. She said, 'All right, darling. We'll go there together.'

horrible thought

I felt so happy, so pleased about Star, about finding her at the airport before she winged it away anywhere, so happy about her being reunited with her mum.

I didn't really think about what might happen after that. I didn't want to think a horrible thought.

My mother, bird of ill omen, said grimly as she sliced onions for dinner, 'What will they say to the father? Things won't be that simple for your friend Star.'

YES THEY WILL! I WANT THEM TO BE SIMPLE!

Sum–sum–summertime

No stress, no exams, no nagging about Urly Nites by the parents.

Mind you, it got off to a bad start.

Star and her mum took lots of very deep breaths and went round to talk to her dad.

'It was nightmarish!' Star told me. 'They ended up screaming and shrieking at each other. They accused each other of abandoning me! They shrieked about my self-image and how I perceived this and that, until I just told them to SHUT UP! They were making it far worse than it was just to score points. I had to calm them down, M, and tell them that neither of them had abandoned me. It's guilt, you see, guilt at a broken marriage. And it wasn't made better knowing that Lynn and her kids could probably hear every word.' She shuddered. 'Still, I think I have reassured them now. I am going to be with Mum for a while at least.'

Star and her mum booked into a Bed and Breakfast for a while. Lizzie and I went visiting. I'd never been to a B and B before. I thought it was a bit like a dolls' house, all pink duvets and white and gold china dogs (probably stocked by Top Bob).

My mother persuaded them to stay a couple of nights at our house too, and that was great. We had never had much contact with Star's family before. Star's mum is a bit strange. Nice strange. My mother says she's unworldly. Mmm, not a bad description. But I like her, especially because she's Star's mum.

She said to Star, 'You'll get to go on a plane after all. I've booked us a couple of weeks. We'll see those islands in the Aegean.'

Star threw her arms round her mum and they both held on tight. I'd never seen Star all fluid and cuddly like this before. Usually she was a bit wooden in the body department.

Then she drew back to smile at her mum and said,

'Maybe one of these summers, I'll go to Greece with M and Lizzie!'

'Yeah!' we screamed.

More of that in a year or two, when the dream becomes reality.

salad bowl suntan

Lizzie and I did much sunbathing. She went the same brown as our olive wood salad bowl.

I went red. I felt sulky. But I put on pounds worth of before and after sun stuff and at last I went a sort of reddy-gold that went perfectly with pale pearly varnish on the toenails. I imagined my toes, gold against bleached sand, while a gorgeous man lurked in the palm trees, ready to bring me a golden drink in a frosted glass with one of those little parasol things, and maraschino cherries. Lizzie began working at the Good Looking Café on Saturdays. I went in once or twice for a chocolate milkshake. I liked having Lizzie to wait on me! I kept changing my mind about what I wanted, just to wind her up, because I always want chocolate milkshake.

I also spied on Real Genuine Craig in the sports shop one Saturday, when I was looking at trainers. I decided he was quite good looking, tall and dark, but sad around the eyes. What were we going to do about Star and him? Nothing, because she was away with her mum.

And me?

Walking with Basil one afternoon, I spied a card in Bob's window, just above the leeks,

shop assistant for few hours each week.

'Basil, sorry, walk interrupted,' I said. I wouldn't be able to concentrate on the interview with him howling at the shop door.

'Where are you going, Emma, all so smart?' called my mother who never misses anything, especially if you don't want her to see it.

'For a job,' I said. 'Top girl at Top Bob's.'

'Do you want me to come with you?' she asked.

What? *No way*!

'It's just that I could ask about the money, Emma. They may not pay you enough. It's your right as a young female to be paid, not exploi –'

I slammed the door shut. My mother still floats about in a geriatric feminist fug (but at least she wears a bra instead of flopping about like a pair of old party balloons like some I have seen).

Thinking, money money money, I hurried back to Bob's. I knew he was there because the pink and silver Bobmobile was outside.

I said, 'Please may I speak to someone about the summer job?'

The copper-haired ladies exchanged looks. One of them said, 'Mr Bob is in today as it happens. He's in the back. I'll see if he has a moment.'

I heard whispering from the back. Then *clack clack*

clackety clack and out came Mr Bob.

I said, 'Erm I saw the erm advert erm and I would like to erm work here. Over the summer holidays, please. I am erm a frequent customer.'

Mr Bob smelled of fabric softener, or tumble-drier tumbler helper, or something sweet and cleaning. He wore a silky lilac shirt and one of those thin ties like liquorice strings that seedy cowboys wear when they chat up gin-voiced blondes down the saloon.

Mr Bob said, 'Yes, dear, I've seen you in here. But I don't want that dog anywhere near, dear.'

At once I felt *confrontational*.

'What's your name, dear?'

'Emma. Emma Peek.'

'Age, dear?'

'Sixteen. I've just finished my exams and I would like to work for a few hours every week.' A light was switched on – make that two lights – behind Mr Bob's gold-rimmed glasses.

Were they pound signs?

'And you live local, dear? You wouldn't be late for work, would you?'

'I'm only five minutes down the road.'

'Still living at home?'

'Yes.'

'Good. You see, I am short-staffed. I have been let down. I have to serve in the shop myself sometimes. And with the school holidays coming up it's difficult for some of my ladies to work. We could take you on for a few hours each morning.'

SKANKY PANTS! My body clock is not programmed for an early start, especially when I should be recovering from the stresses of school.

Mr Bob put his head on one side, like a bird in a copper-coloured hairpiece.

He said, 'I can offer you about ten hours a week, dear.'

I knew I was supposed to think he was doing me a big favour.

'And is that at the minimum wage, please, Mr Bob?'

There! I'd said it! I could feel my face turning red as the rind of the Edam cheese in his cool cabinet, and the sweat breaking out under my BIG TROUBLE T-shirt.

But you see, the alternative was my mother stomping up the road, bottom juddering, to harangue Mr Bob about my rates of pay.

Worst nightmare scenario! My mother in full feminist rant! The shame, the humiliation . . .

That's why I said it myself, even if I didn't say it very loudly. *Minimum wage.*

He definitely went off me a bit then, did Mr Bob. His eyes behind their glasses went sort of flat.

The little lights dimmed fast.

He said, 'Mmm. Well. Er.'

Then the light came back on. Glimmer!

'Let's start with a few hours on Friday morning, dear. Eight till twelve.'

Aagh!

toil and travail

Hard work? Back-breaking toil and travail? Let me tell you about it.

It wasn't just mornings I had to do. There were some afternoons too, and there were even Saturday evenings *and* I had to wear an overall, produced by the copper-haired ladies. It was white and shapeless, with striped trimmings, like a deckchair. My mother kept washing it, insisting it should be whiter than a polo mint, which didn't really go with her liberated woman bit.

If I am honest, one of the lures about a job in Bob's was my fantasy of discount chocolate, but I think I waved that one goodbye when I squeaked 'minimum wage'.

There was little or no spare time for chocolate consumption, believe me! I had to label things and dust and stock shelves and be at the grabready for Mr Bob's microbargain suppers.

Let me explain. If any microwave meals for one were past their sell-by date by the splitness of a second, I had to swoop down and put them aside for Mr Bob. He ate alone. He lacked female company. Pram Gran pushed her way into my mind again . . . but that picture wasn't quite right, somehow. Mr Bob was *un poco* miserly, methinks. *El Scroogio.*

He plays music all the time, does Mr Bob. Country and

Western to go with his roody-dude boots, all about blankets on the ground, crops in the field and the Good Lord taking vengeance with beans and little green apples. His speakers crackle and fade and *whooomph*. I thought, Jono Watkins could sort out Mr Bob's sound system for him.

Talking of which . . . or Wot . . .

A Top Bob's babe

Whenever I think of the Unspeakable he seems to appear like some ghastly big genie in combats! He hadn't got any quieter. His foghorn voice boomed out across the shop, 'Hey! Straight out of one uniform and into another! How dazzling white are you, M! A true Bob's babe!'

I was in Top Bob's, not Bottom's, lining up the plastic shepherdesses so they could gaze at that dodgy plaster kingfisher. I remember *All About Kingfishers* from primary school, and I tell you, this plaster one would have been chased off the river, because it was the wrong shape, wrong size, wrong colour, wrong bird.

'Put the budgie down and talk to me,' said Jono, 'because, Emma Peek, you are the answer to my prayer. I'm looking for a goin' away prez for my mum!'

Jono, your mum should have had a present sixteen years ago. Someone else instead of you. They should have switched babies in the hospital and sent you off for research.

Jono was looking reasonable. He'd got a not bad deep blue T-shirt and a bit of a tan. The trouble with Bob's overall is no one can see my golden skin.

I said, 'What have you in mind, Jono? Where is your mum going away to?'

'Not her, M! I'm the one that's going away. I'm going off to Europe with Luke, Ash and a couple of sixth form dudes. We're gonna follow in the footsteps of the cool.'

'Well, watch out for donkey muck, Jono. So you're not having another party?'

What was that little sinking feeling in my stomach? Disappointment. You see, secretly I had dreamed of performing my full catering repertoire if he were to host another Unspeakable Thrash. I would throw in a few chocolate truffles and pizzarettes (see below) to give it all some class.

HANDS–FREE PIZZARETTES

Your mother will need
- **225g pizza flour**
- **packet of dried yeast**
- **bit of olive oil, salt, maybe an egg, let her feel empowered by these small choices**

Leave your mother happily mixing up this pizza dough. Tell her the olive oil is good for her crêpey hands. Indulge her as she kneads and stretches and thumps. She likes doing it, it takes out her middle-aged frustrations and

---

slows down the onset of her arthritis. And you won't get sticky hands, or have to stay in all Saturday while it rises. She can stay in the warm kitchen until the dough rises. Then get her to roll it into thin, thin circles. Then you do the fun decorating bit!

You will need
- **tomato sauce**
- **your favourite cheese, which is mozzarella if you're making it for Lizzie cos she likes real Italian**
- **olives and capers and little salty anchovies and any other bits you like, red and orange pepper strips perhaps**
- **Sprinkle it with chopped oregano (more real italian)**

Make it PRETTY!
Bake it HOT! *OVEN GLOVE ALERT.*

The base is much much nicer than shop ones, but don't tell your mother or she'll get bigheaded.

'Aw, sorry M babe, no summer party is planned. Band crisis. Mass Devastation is no more.'

I almost took pity on him! *Almost* . . . His face was a bit crumpled and fallen, as far as Jono's face could ever fall.

'What will you do without a band, Jono?'

'Oh, there's still a band, babe, but now we're called Nobody's Heroes.'

Hmmm . . .

He switched his usual Watkins grin back on and said, 'Maybe a party in the autumn? Sorry to make you lose out on a summer one, M.'

'Don't be sorry, Jono. I've got lots of parties lined up. And be careful you don't drop those figurines −' because he was moving china cows and robins and gold-edged ladies around, turning them upside down, even! He waved a bunch of artificial flowers, tweaked the hands of a (gold, I don't think so) clock. He tried to wrench a china orange out of its bowl. He was a shopkeeper's nightmare.

In the end he settled for a snowstorm. Inside was a smiling snowman with a carrot nose. It looked rather like him. It wore a black Fedora hat, and kept getting smothered in silver stars when you turned it upside down. I think it was left over from Mr Bob's Christmas extravaganza.

'Jono,' I said. 'It's July.'

'But she likes things like this. She's a child at heart. Where's the Drama Dudesse today?'

'She's working in the coffee house in town. She's off for a Theatre Fortnight soon.'

'Oh yeah. She told me she's goin' to stage school next term. Bit posh, innit? How is Star?'

'She's gone to a Greek island with her mum, don't know which one. Something with soss on the end. Or maybe it was Crete.'

I wonder if she ever did anything about Real Craig's

letter? Did she access him? Jono Watkins did not know about Craig. Hee hee hee!

He went on, 'And then what? Will Star come back to England again for school?'

Horror! I hadn't let myself think about that . . .

'I don't know! Oh, I hope so!' I cried.

'Well she's not going back to her dad's, is she? She was miserable there. And her mum works in France. When I saw her at your place with her mum, I thought, Yes! that's right for you, Star! you've lost all that restless, sad stuff. You see,' proclaimed the Unspeakable, 'I've got like an extra sense about people. I get to know what they're feeling.'

He stared into my eyes.

Well, Jono, I'm feeling get off my case, Boastie Boy!

I stared right back but he just grinned, he's Unsquashable as well as Unspeakable.

He said, 'I was real worried about Star. And you know who else? Cath. Every time I see her she's on her own. Why doesn't she tag along with you girlies?'

'Because she's horrible.'

He shrugged. He said, 'You three would sort her out. She says she's got no friends.'

He paid for his skanky snowstorm and a soppy pink card and called, 'See ya in the Big Six. Have a good summer, babe. Oh, and tell Bottom Bob his sounds are *awful*.'

'You have a good summer too, Jono,' I called and he turned and grinned.

I watched him barge across to the stairs and listened as he crashed out.

He had thrown me into panic and despair. What if next term there was no Star? No Lizzie? Horrible thought.

How would I ever live?

That night, I told Basil all about it. He stared deep into my eyes. Then he yawned with a funny little squeaking noise.

Sometimes I look at Basil and I wonder about the big questions in life, you know, God and natural selection and fate and all that stuff.

I mean, whatever put Basil together? He's like all different bits put together in a game of consequences, with an anteater nose, Dachshund body, Doberman black and tan colouring, fox tail, hedgehog legs, cheesy Hobbit feet, Robbie Williams eyes and Afro fur.

Is he All Chance? Random Dog? Is he Meant to Be? Or did he Just Happen, a small Dog Accident?

Does the Divine Light shine in Basil?

I mean, he very nearly wasn't here at all. If we hadn't rescued him from the Homeless Kennels it would have been Night Night Basil!

'Life keeps changing, Basil, all the time. We go our different ways. What do you think of that?' Basil didn't bother to consider. He changed into a curly furry fossil and went fast asleep.

Gross grades

My mother announced that she had booked a holiday. For *all* of us.

She said it was a good deal. She said she had spotted it in the travel agent's window.

She waved a brochure at me.

I have to admit it looked good. Spain. A hotel, not too much like a factory, with pools and massages and stuff and hopefully lots of things for Sophie and Sarah to do, kids' clubs with screaming and sploshing paint around, a long long way away from me.

BUT how would I get my exam results?

I rushed off to see Lizzie in the GLC. There she was, in her pinny and that sort of little white beak thing on her head. I would have looked like a pigeon, but Lizzie looked good.

'Lizzie,' I said, 'will you collect my results, and I'll ring you up and ask you, and you tell me unless they are too terrible. Then you say Gross Grades. No, wait . . . someone might be tapping the phone. You say GG. That's code, for Gross Grades. That means I wait to find out when I get home.'

Lizzie was being Scarlett O'Hara that particular afternoon, even though she was wearing a beak. She'd got her lips sort of pursed up Deep South style, her profile Southern Belle and she kept tossing back her head so that I feared for the safety of the little white beak. She put down my chocolate milkshake and said, 'I think that can be arranged, Missy Emma. I'll be back by then, long

long way back from Theatre Fortnight.'

She sorted the bowl of sugar sticks, staring hard at Good Looking the Youngest. He was melting the heart of a Pretend Old Redhead by sprinkling extra chocolate on her cappuccino.

'If he doesn't stop chatting up everything in a skirt, he can go sleep with the fishes,' snarled Lizzie. 'Cheat on me, and frankly, Mr Enrico, *I don't give a damn!*'

She tossed her head and said, 'That's from *Gone with the Wind*, M. I'm Scarlett O'Hara.'

'Yes, but Rhett Gable says that bit, Lizzie. It wasn't Scarlett O'Hara.'

'Doesn't matter,' she sniffed. 'My art may lead me across gender boundaries.'

Hmmm.

'Hey, Great Uncle Roberto is looking dapper today,' I said. 'Look, he's got legs!'

Great Uncle Roberto was out from behind the counter. He was not very tall, but his height was helped by the great huge hair sweeping up from his noble forehead.

He wore black patent shoes with pointed toes. He had a shirt of humbug stripes and a red silky tie. He was up and strutting around like a little lord. Had he been rejuvenated? Face-lifted? Freeze-dried? He looked years younger, only about eighty-nine.

As I watched, his face broke into a wide smile and he held out his hands.

For Pram Gran.

Fiat fatale

'Blimey!' screeched Lizzie, ejected from her Scarlett O'Hara persona. 'Pram Gran has been re-upholstered!'

She certainly had! She wore her hair up in a silver croissant and had a smile as wide as a bandstand. Her short-sleeved jumper was made of pale pink angora fluffy stuff that made you want to cuddle her. Her eyes shone, blue as cornflowers. Great Uncle Roberto took her hand and kissed it with a great huge smacking sound and his tidal wave wobbled.

'Lizzie! Pram Gran looks like a *femme fatale*. Do you think Great Uncle Roberto and Pram Gran are an item?'

'I think they're going to be,' said Lizzie knowingly.

'He looks as if he wants to whisk her away on his gondola, or his red Lamborghini,' I said.

How could I ever have thought of her fixed up with Meany Mr Bob? I could see now that she wasn't a Cadillac woman at all. And Mr Bob wasn't a dog fan. He had never wanted to get to know my Basil. I wondered if Great Uncle Roberto liked dogs?

Never mind. I think he was replacing one.

You never can tell with people, can you? There's more to life than meets the something or other. That's another thing to embroider on your sampler along with the lemon cake wisdom.

Then Lizzie said, 'He won't whisk her off into the sunset in a red Ferrari, M. Great Uncle Roberto drives a little Fiat. It's white and it's rusty.'

wicked woman

So summer ambled along. Lizzie went off on her dramatic fortnight, Star was still away somewhere, even the Unspeakable was absent. I worked in Bob's *really really hard* and read and sat in the sunshine with Basil while my sisters wrestled in their inflatable pool.

'I'm sorry you have to go in the kennels, Basil,' I told him. 'But you can't come to Spain. It's too hot for someone as hairy as you. And the silly hotel does not take dogs.'

Basil rolled his eyes, then thoughtfully placed a bit of chomped onion on my sunkissed knee.

'Put that spade down, Sarah!' screeched my mother, tramping across the grass.

'Hey, Mum, when do I get new clothes for the holiday?' I drawled.

'Emma, I've just spent a fortune on your new sixth form stuff, and more school shoes because you say you can have higher heels in the sixth. You don't need more holiday clothes too!'

'I do! I need a white top for my tan and a new bikini.'

'You've *got* a bikini! And you've got a holiday job to earn money for extra clothes!'

'But I've got so many expenses. And I need cleanser. And my allowance was never supposed to cover under-wear, or shoes, or essentials such as bikinis!'

My mother sighed. She said, 'Spend, spend . . . and those two need more shorts and things and I still haven't rung the vet.'

I was up and at her! 'Why are you ringing the vet? You're not really going to make Basil have that operation!'

'What operation?' cried big ears Sophie.

My mother stared down into the grass as if she had just noticed a parallel universe.

'Oh . . . just something boy dogs have done.'

Sarah and Sophie stood before ·her, dripping. They weren't going to move without an answer.

Sarah reached for Sophie's hand. *As if.*

My mother said, 'We don't want Basil to be a daddy, do we?'

'Ooh! Yes we do!' screamed Sarah, jumping up and down. 'Baby Basils. We can keep them all. But who·will be the mum?'

'No, Sarah. There are too many dogs in the world already.'

'No there aren't!'

'People don't want the Basil sort.'

'*We* do! Mixcha Dogs are the best!'

'Sarah, listen to me. If there are too many puppies they end up at the Dogs' Home. And if nobody wants them they get put to sleep. So we don't want Basil to be a daddy, so . . .'

'So you're having his lumps cut off, aren't you!' shouted Sophie. 'You cruel and wicked woman!'

Sarah turned a bone-white face to me. 'Does she mean his potatoes?'

'His testicles. Yes. I'm afraid so.'

Sarah's lip began to quiver. A tear rolled down her cheek and plopped on to Basil's back. Sophie stormed down to the bottom of the garden and scrambled up her sulking tree. My mother ran indoors.

No bus to Borneo

I had to get up the next morning even though it wasn't a Bob day, but stress doesn't just end when exams are over, you see, and if I wanted a decent Parental Contribution towards more clothes, I knew I'd have to go shopping *con mi familia*.

It took ages. Sophie threw a tantrum and ran off into the market because she could only have two pairs of shorts. Sarah kept saying, 'Testicles . . . Testicles . . .' and doing a little dance.

My mother moaned on about coffee and horrible public loos. And of course there was a lot of Mother Mutter in the shops, although she is better nowadays about keeping out of the way until it is time for her to pay.

I got a pink bikini, some aquamarine shorts and a white strappy top! Not bad, eh?

Trouble was, in the changing room mirror I seemed to go straight from the top bit to the bottom, like a great huge tree trunk. No waist any more. The bit in the middle didn't go in to make room for the air. There was too much of me. *Heffa moose! Socorro!* I wouldn't look slinky round the hotel pool. Less chocolate, more exercise.

So the next afternoon I went swimming. I caught a bus to the public pool. I took my skanky old black school cozzie. I wasn't going to show off my porkiness in my new bikini or risk chlorine damage to it.

And no, I did not take my sisters. 'Not today, Mum, I need to do thirty lengths!' I shouted. 'Maybe another time,' and *vroom*! I was out of the front door fast.

All right, it was only thirteen lengths, with breaks in between while I clung wheezing to the bar. But I resisted the crisp and fizz machine. Why do they always put gleaming machines full of unhealthy stuff for when you come starving out of the pool?

I felt *mucho* smug and virtuous. I was going to look good in my new pink bikini in Spain. I was all warm with exercise. I must be skinny already, I thought as the bus purred homewards.

And then, just when you think you know the way home and it's always the same, I heard this voice.

'May I sit here?'

wing yip and panic stations and up to the penthouse in a waste bin!

'Oh – yes – course,' I stammered. At least, I think that's what I said.

My mind was a wire mesh waste bin, all overturned, and thoughts like little scraps of paper were whirling round it! *It's him! Beautiful Stranger! Blond Boy! Almost Craig!*

And other scraps screamed, *Hope I don't stink of chlorine, I splatted on lots and lots of shower stuff didn't I, and splodged loads and loads of conditioner on the bunny hair, and I have perfect toenails in Sugar Snap Green just in case he drops his ticket and has to grovel on the floor and comes face to foot with my feet . . .*

I gabbled, 'I see you from my school bus!'

Cool? Maybe not. But I'm Emma Peek.

He said, 'Do you?'

'Yes. Waiting in the mornings. Do you work round here?'

'I do. But I won't have to bus it much more. I'm getting wheels in September, part of my training package!'

He had a soft voice and such elegant clothes, I thought, sneaking a look at his I-don't-care-Oh-so-casual-but-I'm-dead-smart cotton suit.

The waste bin was still spinning fast but I had to find out quick!

I asked, 'What do you train for?'

'Oh, I'm working in my dad's business. Travel.'

'Ooh, that sounds good.'

'It will be. I'm off to Borneo in the autumn to investigate the prospects there.'

Borneo? I don't think there's a bus to Borneo.

He said, 'So will you be going back to school?'

'Yes. The sixth form. That's as long as I don't completely flunk my exams.'

'And then?'

I shrugged. 'I don't know. I quite like most subjects, but I'm not brilliant at anything.'

'I should do the subjects you enjoy,' he said.

Good advice, I thought. I told him, 'I don't know what I'll do for a job. I want to go to – maybe I want to go away to art college. Except I wouldn't want to leave Basil.'

'Is that your boyfriend, or your brother?'

'It's my dog.'

He threw back his head and laughed. 'What? Oh, come on, it's only a dog!'

I asked him, 'So what will you do in Borneo? They have orang-utans, don't they?'

'Yes. Believe it or not, some people like them. I would investigate the feasability of eco-tourism,' he said, gazing ahead. 'That's the thing of the future. I shall see what the place can offer, in terms of archaeology, cave art, wildlife, local festivals and food. And then I'd plan the operation. It's a fast-growing market. A market for the better off discerning customer who wants something different . . .'

He stood up. He said, 'I've got to catch another bus here. I'm going to see someone on business. See you around. Hope your results are brilliant.'

'Thank you.' His eyes were not quite as deep brown as I thought. Hazelnut brown, maybe . . . They certainly weren't organic plain chocolate, melting over heat. That's what I had hoped for. They were just brown.

'What's your name?' he asked.

'Emma. Emma Peek.'

'Hello, Emma Peek. I'm Daniel. Daniel Draper. See you around.'

I watched him walk away from the bus. After five steps he turned and smiled.

For a very long time I was speechless.

That was partly because I had nobody to speak to.

When I got home I went to my room because I wanted to be Alone, yes, a touch of the Greta Garbos, and think about him. I searched for *The Daily Sightings*. It seemed years since I had been able to write anything in there! Daniel Draper. DD. I like writing when the subject is so very special. I had to keep pushing Basil away so I could get on with it.

I did some pencil sketches, too.

Travel? Cave art? Borneo? Eco-tourism and orang-utans? I like orang-utans. They have beautiful weird faces but their eyes make me sad. Would they like eco-tourism, people watching them build their big leafy nests and going to sleep? Words whirled round in my head, all these things I'd never even heard of before. He was going for success, that one, and he was so cool and confident. I played that scene over and over again in my head. I thought about him, the Beautiful Stranger, now that I had finally met him.

But I tell you something . . . I'm sure I saw dark roots in his hair.

Las vacaciones en España

The holiday in Spain?

I have to admit I loved it. I even said thank you to my mother at one o'clock one morning. There was sun, sand, sea, and sangria, *pollo con pomfrittes con paella*, lots of OK people my age to chat to and meet up with by the pool or on the beach for a barbecue.

There was a really fit waiter called Pedro.

There was a chunky monkey diving teacher called Paulo.

My dear little sisters were thoroughly happy ELSEWHERE so everybody had a good time.

We came back the very last evening of the holidays, the night before school, just in time to collect Basil from the kennels. He had pulled all the tufty bits out from between his toes. Boredom, I suppose. Maybe he was pining . . .

Basil! *Un momento* . . . there is one wonderful thing I forgot to tell you!

Reprieve! Reprieve and temporary pardon for Basil!

The day after the *Tears in the Paddling Pool* episode, my mother mumbled that there wouldn't be time for Basil to have his op and recover before we went abroad. She said he might need nursing and feeding by hand with lightly cooked chicken. He would need a lot of sitting on knees. He couldn't do that in the kennels. So the op was off!

My father shouted, 'You're safe this time, Old Boy!' and thumped Basil on the back.

Wag that tail, mi bonito perro.

Basil was a happy dog, home from the kennels. He found a soggy broad bean pod in the compost heap and carried it everywhere. He tore round and round the garden in circles, so ecstatic to be back here, and not find himself back at the dog's home.

I wasn't ecstatic. I don't like coming back after a holiday. It's cold. Goosepimples breed all over you. Your room looks a minging mess, there's no fresh bread, and no after sun left to nourish your golden body. The only pads you can find are great huge heffa moose hammocks for squirrels, because it was your father who was sent shopping just before you went away and he has NO IDEA! The house smells from being shut up and all your underwear needs washing. Your mother needs to get her finger out *pronto*, but all the woman does is fall into a chair and open a bottle of Spanish wine.

There was a postcard from Lizzie on her theatre course, saying I AM EXHAUSTED! in gold pen, and a card from Star, of beautiful blue and green sea, telling me all about a visit to some sunbaked old stones.

Oh, by the way, when I rang Lizzie from Spain she told me my exam results were dead good, much better than I ever thought they would be. Lizzie's results were good, too. I'm pleased, I feel smug. But things aren't that different just because I've got GCSEs. My sisters still fight. I don't look any different. My hair is still unruly and I love chocolate more than ever.

And there is one new Unanswered Universal Question from my holiday. Why, oh why, do the labels on men's swimming trunks always stick up just above their bottom crack?

This summer just gone

So the summer has gone now. It's still warm, but the nights are drawing in. Life revs up again. It's a new term, and it's timetables and getting up in the mornings.

I don't feel real. I'm ever so brown! I've never been so brown in my whole life, and my hair has got blonde bits in. I bought loads of lemons. They were cheap because they have loads of lemons in Spain. I squeezed lemon juice all over my hair and sat in the sun and I think that helped it bleach. Sticky factor? High. I had a lot of flies *brrrm*ing round my head.

Return ticket, please

I'm on the bus again. It seems an age since I sat on these blue and red seats. It's hard to imagine that the bus has been *brrrm whoosh hiss*ing all this time without us.

I smooth down my smart dark skirt. I admire my golden-brown knees and my legs all glossed up with after sun. My glossy legs end in smart black shoes with stacked heels. They're new. They're clean and shiny, today, anyway. I think, clean shoes look elegant.

I wonder if we keep shoe polish at home?

Inside my elegant new shoes are very brown, elegant feet.

My toenails are equally impressive. They're all the same! Every single one of them is shell-pink. It looks good with the tan.

I feel smart. I never feel smart. I do today.

There's no Boss Woman on the bus.

Something is going *ahem*! and whistling loudly behind me. It is clearly something that wants to be noticed, and so of course I don't, I ignore the *ahems* and whistles as long as I can, which is about two seconds, because I am a student of Life and I like to know what is going on. It's lively curiosity about my fellow human beings. It's not nosiness as *some* might think.

I turn round.

It should be Jono Watkins, but something's not quite right. Quite a few things aren't quite right! The face is light golden brown. There are no spots or even spot craters, that I can see – all right, I'm a couple of seats away, so maybe there are spot remains if you get out a magnifying glass, but from here it looks as if the sun has blasted all spot life clean away. His eyes look blue, cornflower blue, blue yolks, I mean middles, blue irises, with proper white surrounds. There's a touch of cunning blond stubble. Someone who can cut has been at his hair.

The scarecrow look has gone. His hair has real sun in it.

Is it Jono, or some kind of audition? If it's an Unspeakable audition, this one gets the part.

'So where did you get that suntan, Emma Peek?' goes the Unspeakable Look Alike.

'*My* suntan, Jono? I got mine in Spain.'

'And did you meet a cool dude so you can boast about him to the babes?'

It really *is* Jono Watkins. It is unmistakably the Unspeakable. No one else has such pathetic people skills. 'Jono, I met not one, but two cool dudes. A very luscious diving instructor. His name was Paulo. He wanted to give me free lessons. And there was Pedro the head waiter who kept pouring me only the very best sangria.'

He stares at me as if I am exaggerating. Cheek! He needs putting down, he always needs putting down, with or without a suntan, but he just won't be *put*!

I tell him, 'Stop calling us babes, Jono! It's sexist, and so patronising!' but he doesn't take it up, he just laughs his snorty laugh and shouts, 'Pedro! That's a donkey's name! Did he have a big straw hat with holes for his ears? Did you give him a carrot?'

Ho Ho Ho Jono Watkins. So unfunny. Some things in life don't change, do they? I'm not giving up, so I tell him, 'Paulo took me out on his top of the range speedboat.'

So stick that in your melon crocodile! He goes quiet for a second or two.

Now, was it Pedro, or Paulo . . . *Yo no puedo recordar.*

Who's at the bus stop now?

I feel as if I'm in a dream as we *brrrm whoosh hiss* along.

I haven't got used to being back in England yet. I don't know who will get on this bus. It's the same as it was, but different from last term. People still make *grump humph* noises even when you're in the sixth form.

I phoned Lizzie last night but there was no reply.

I feel a bit nervous. I tell myself that's silly. But for the past five years I have looked forward to starting each term, not because of *work*, although I do like some of it. I have to tell you I got some good grades! *Yes, Me, Emma Peek, I got A★ for art, and A★ for history and A for English*!!!!!!!! Boast, boast! All right, so the sciences were *un poco* disappointing. I'm not retaking them, I can live without science. Other people can do science. They are called scientists. My French grade could have been much better, if I was much better at French.

But my exams were fine. They're finished, and I'm not dead, my house is still standing and my feet look just as fine as ever.

Back to the point . . . I've looked forward to going back to school over the past five years because that is where I see my friends.

Today I don't even know if my best friends will be there.

My heart is stuck halfway between the penthouse and the first floor. I think it's in my throat.

The Unspeakable is in his zone, but there's no Star

running for the bus although I keep watch for her long before the bus pulls up at her stop.

Efcharisto, George

You never know who will be at the next stop. Or who won't be there, either.

I've tried to tell myself that Star is in France with her mum now, but this morning I know that most of me has hoped against hope she'd be back and going to school again with me.

Now I hold my breath waiting for the next dreadful thing.

It doesn't happen! Because bursting on to the bus, shouting, 'Hi Steve! How's the Wife?' is *LIZZIE*!!!!!!!

'I thought you were off to stage school!' I shout.

'The Patriarch said it was too expensive,' she says. 'He said, "You've got a good drama lot at your real school, Elizabeth, never mind all that arty-farty-airy-fairy stuff at this stage place!"' *Efcharisto*, George! But I had better try to turn down my smile a bit and seem sympathetic.

'Oh, Lizzie, I'm really sorry. Were you very upset?'

'No. I didn't want to go there anyway, not after the Theatre Fortnight. It was full of snotty little rich posers. There were no fit boys that I could see, not one. And I didn't think they did anything better than our theatre studies do. So I'm coming back to school with you lot!' she screams and flings her arms round me, as much as the bus seat will let her and gives me a great huge hug.

'Oi! Lizzie Astopoulis! bring some of that down here!' roars the Unspeakable.

'Hello, Jono! Good to see you!' shrieks Lizzie, and – yes – she staggers down the bus to give him a hug too. I don't know what to think! Then she's back up the bus to plant a big smacker on the head of . . . Tuba Boy! Only he's not . . .

Tuba Boy, who is not any more

Tuba Boy has not got a tuba. No. His case this morning is smaller. It is still too large to take easily on the bus, but it is not as huge as his tuba. Tuba Boy himself is taller. He has spent the summer in a Gro-bag.

'What's that?' screeches Lizzie, pointing.

'Saxophone,' he mutters, face suddenly Szechuan red because a Big Girl has paid him some Attention. Guess what! Not only has he graduated to saxophone, his voice has gone all down to bass, deep and gruff. Is he putting it on? He looks surprised by it too. I guess it's just the old hormones pulling the voice down towards his feet.

As we move away from the stop I remember to look for someone. He's not there.

Dodo Dollop lives!

We get off the bus just as a powder-blue car draws up by the school gate. Dodo Dollop climbs out, bending down to kiss the driver. He's there a while.

I say, 'So Dodo has got himself a life at last. And he's got the same initials!'

'Who has?'

'Dodo Dollop has the same initials as Daniel Draper. The Beautiful Stranger. I met him in the end. Fancy Dodo and him having the same initials, double D!'

'Do you two ever talk about anything else? Nothing but guys guys guys. And it's TD, really, M, not DD.'

'You're just jealous cos we don't talk about you, Jono Watkins!'

He just laughs. Why isn't he cross? Why doesn't he flounce away and sulk?

And then I look at him again. You know, he's not quite as Unspeakable as he was.

The Wot Kin are gathering. There's Ashad, all dark jowls. He must shave ten times a day. He's even hairier than Basil. He's all scowly and hostile, and smouldering eyes, but I know it's because he's nervous, because I have known Ashad for years.

I realise that Ashad is quite fit, even though he is an everyday thing.

And there's Dean, smiling like a little kid. His suit's too big for him. His mum wants it to last. Aw! That's sweet. Tunde strolls up, all sophisticated, tall and gold-rimmed and serious as a bank manager, but when I find out his results later on, I realise he'll be more than the manager of your corner bank, he'll be Chief Economic Bigtime Bod reporting to the government. Except he says he's dead keen to do stuff in the Third World and get rid of the debt that makes everyone poor.

And then it happens.

OW-WUH! I go right over on one ankle and come out of my elegant new shoes.

Well, if you must know, I got half a size too big, because they hadn't got a pair of sevens in stock and I loved that style, and I had a great huge job on to make my mother buy them at all, and she had to do the Mother Mutter, I told you so, Emma, but you always know best and you can't walk in shoes big as boats. All that scabby Mother Mutter parent paranoia. I suppose she thinks she's only doing her job. But now it's Aaagh! PANIC ATTACK! because the Unspeakable rushes to pick up the boat – I mean, shoe.

He goes, 'I've got your shoe, Emma. Come on, now.'

He's gone down on one knee – well, almost, he doesn't want to get his new chuddies mucky – so he's wobbling but still balanced and is holding out the shoe for me to put on.

And then I lose it and open my mouth when I shouldn't!

'If you must know I wash them at least twice a day!'

'Eh? What are you talking about?'

'Don't act so ignorant! I'm talking feet, Jono, I'm talking

trainers. You know perfectly well what I'm talking about. That party when you made a great huge fuss about my feet smelling. That party in Year Seven with hot dogs when Adam was sick in the rubber plant. It was hot and I had old trainers.'

I've said it and I wish I hadn't, but I do open my mouth and put my foot right in it sometimes and now I think I might cry.

'All I remember from the party is a smelly old cat,' he says, grabbing my foot and sliding on the shoe. 'There, Cinderella. Try not to fall down again, clumsy woman!'

He straightens up, and strolls after his mob.

And I realise at last that he doesn't remember my smelly feet.

THE CHEAT! After all these years. How could he be so . . . so . . . Jono Watkins?

'Come on, M,' says Lizzie, 'let's go and find everyone.'

We have our own room now, all of us sixth formers. We don't have to mingle with children or pubescents if we don't want to. I am going to do art, and English and history.

Do you know, I am looking forward to it.

On the way to the sixth (must get used to calling it that) we see Dodo. He is all in crisp, parchment-coloured cotton clothing, smart as a catalogue man, except for his nose, of course, no male model would have that hooter. Well, I wonder who chose his clothes!

He says, 'Very well done, Emma. Congratulations. A pleasant surprise in English, wasn't it? And Lizzie! I know the drama department is pleased you're staying on with us. Of course, I always knew my form would do brilliantly.'

'Good to see you too, sir.' And do you know, it really is. Dear old Dodo Dollop. 'How is your er −'

'Karen? Oh she's fine. She's just on her way to the council offices now. She's in charge of Highways and Byways, you know,' he smirks.

WHAT? In those shoes?

'But can't you be head of our sixth, Mr Donaldson?' pleads Lizzie.

Dodo goes all pink and pleased. 'Oh, come along now girls, you've got Mrs Conway,' he says. 'She's very − er − brisk and efficient.' Yes, Dodo, you've just confirmed our worst fears.

We open the door. Lots of faces turn to look at us. Lots of our old form, and some new people come in from other schools. They look terrified. There's Cath Ratcliffe, of course. She looks just like Cath Ratcliffe, terrified too.

I suddenly feel tall and confident and kinda sixth formy with my smart shoes and my grades and my double D notes. I stroll over (not too casual because I don't trust my boats) and I say, 'Hi, Cath. Had a good summer?'

She gives a little jump and then she says, 'Ooh, hi, M. Er − the summer was all right, thank you.'

She's gone pink, I think she's surprised someone has said hello to her. So am I.

The room is quite big, and it's got armchairs and a CD player in case you can ever all agree about what to play, and a drinks machine that makes thin drinks in pollies.

I look round at all the faces, all waiting, all wondering what the new times bring.

I feel old but happy. Guess what? I am going to have to bake Great Huge Cookies one day soon by way of celebration so quick, here's the recipe.

GREAT HUGE COOKIES (WITH JUST A JUST A HINT OF GINGER) (MAKE AT LEAST THREE LOTS TO BE ENOUGH FOR YOUR CLASS)

You will need
- **Self–raising flour – about 220g**
- **Sugar, about 2 big spoons of it, for texture's sake**
- **100g marg or butter**
- **2 big teaspoons of dried ginger**
- **2 little tiny pinches of cinnamon cos it smells lovely in the oven**
- **4 great huge spoonfuls of golden syrup!**
- **Bit of bicarbonate of soda (your mother will find it)**

1. Put all cloudy stuff through a sieve, add sugar, rub in marg till crummy crumbly. You can warm the golden syrup a bit and then pour it in all dribbly . . . mmmmm! Handle it.
2. Roll it into little tiny balls and put them on some big greased baking thing WITH LOTS OF ROOM BETWEEN THEM, THEY DON'T LIKE OVERCROWDING. Or else you get one very great huge cookie.

---

3. Squidge them ever so lightly with the back of a fork. This flattens them a bit, but I bet it wouldn't work on Jono Watkins.
4. Cook at 5 or 190°C for about 10 or 13 minutes. Leave on baking thing for another 10, then oh-so-carefully lift on to a rack to cool. *OVEN GLOVE ALERT.*

Eat as soon as you can (*no problemo . . .*)
Of course, you have to give your sisters some.

Maybe I'll make the cookies tonight? I feel good seeing everyone and new people and wondering how the sixth form will be, except, I do wish . . .

Oh well. I suppose you can't have everything.

different from Dodo

As we feared, Mrs Conway is quite different from Dodo. She wears I-can't-remember-what-they-are-like dark shoes that go *clok clok clockity clok* and a crisp navy tunic and skirt without dog-hair or fluff and she has rose-pink lipstick and I bet she reads *Good Housekeeping* and has no sweet wrappers on the floor of her car and no teaspoons in her compost heap or outrageous music from yesteryear in her CD collection.

I bet we can't tease her like we did Dodo. I bet she won't buy us Zebra Mints.

'Please settle down everyone,' she calls and you know

everyone will and she knows it too.

'I like a calm and composed lower sixth,' she proclaims. 'Now, I don't know all of you, do I? There are some faces I have seen round school, and some completely new. So I think it's best if we stand up one by one and introduce ourselves to everyone.'

I'm glad *I'm* not completely new because it sounds nerve-racking to me and I've been here for five years already.

'Now then . . . who is going to start us off?'

Guess! Who has got a great huge motorway mouth and self-confidence out of all proportion? You're right.

'Well, hello there and good morning, Mrs Conway. Hello, everyone. Let me introduce myself. Jonathan Watkins is the name! Music, maths and cuisine is the game!'

Mrs Conway smiles as if he's cute! She'll learn.

What's that noise? Is there a mouse in the sixth form suite? There certainly will be after we've been in here a week or two with all our crisps and forgotten old snacks.

The door handle is squeaking.

'I was here last year, as most of you know, and . . . hey, what . . .?'

'Go on, dear,' urges Mrs Conway, and I have a nasty feeling she will nurture maternal feelings towards the Unspeakable.

'I think there is a problem, Mrs C,' he says and makes for the door, knocking over his chair as he goes and frightening a new girl who wraps her arms round her head. They probably had nothing like Jono at her old school.

He wrenches open the door.

He stands a moment, then chuckles that Unspeakable chuckle.

He says, 'Hello there, babe! You've made my day! Come on in.'

And round the door, smiling, sidles . . .

'STAR!' screams everyone, clapping and cheering and banging the table, shattering Mrs Conway's calm, composed sixth form atmosphere right from the very beginning.

It's just like the good old Dodo Days.

All change

It's going to take a long time to catch up.

Star looks so gorgeous! Her hair is all braided with gold and copper thread and she can't stop smiling. She even stands differently, I'm sure she does, and I don't care if you say that's silly.

Star looks if she is pleased to be herself at last.

Mrs Conway has a go at us because we won't stop talking. 'Lower sixth, SHOOOSH!' she whoops. What does she expect? What a start! *Dodo where art thou*!

We have to wait till break for the most important part of the morning, The Star Update.

School is the same but different. Everything is changing, but I think we can keep the best bits.

We'll have more exams over the next couple of years at least – ugh! But they are a long long way away. They're not here yet, and there is a lot of life which isn't exams.

In the meantime, it's the important things, friends and

time together. They are the things that we will remember in years to come, not getting A for English, C for maths or G for French.

No! We'll remember L for Lizzie and S for Star, M for Emma. Maybe A for Ashad and Adam, T for Tunde, DD for Dodo Dollop . . . and I suppose we'll even remember JW.

Star update

Star says that her mum hadn't renewed the teaching contract in France even before she came looking for Star. She's promised to do whatever it takes for Star to be happy.

'Both of us know now that we don't want to go it alone again,' says Star. 'We were mad to try. The one thing left to make me happy, now that I know Mum wants me, is to be back at school with you all.'

'Aw! Star, that's great. But what'll happen for dosh?'

'Mum's doing supply teaching. She's looking for a job at a college, and for now we're renting a flat. Not too near Dad and Lynn. We had to go and see him, before we went to Greece. Poor Dad, I know he felt so bad. And I was angry with him, you know, because it didn't work out living there. I know he loves me really. I love him more now I don't live with him, I know that sounds mad. I think he is relieved that he doesn't have to make us all blend together. He pays me more attention now when I visit him. He bought me a book of John Donne poetry!'

'What about Lynn and co?' asked Lizzie.

Star grins at us, all mischievous. 'Oh, I quite like them now I don't have to be with them! It was awful at first. When I visited with Mum, they just would not look at us, would not make eye contact or speak. Karl whistled silly tunes if I tried to speak!'

Star's step-siblings make Sophie and Sarah sound almost cute. I said *almost*.

'And Mum is happy to be back with me and not having to speak French all day. We're looking for a house with a garden. We can even have a dog, M!'

(Mum . . . you know Basil . . . well, if Basil was a dad dog I know someone who would have one of the puppies . . .)

'So I don't know if I'll still be getting the same bus as you two again,' says Star regretfully.

'But I can't have everything. Is Steve still driving it? What about Tuba Boy, and Pram Gran? And, ooh, Lizzie, tell me how it's been working at the Good Lookings!'

'I'll tell you about the Good Lookings, Star, when you've told me all about meeting up with Genuine Craig,' cries Lizzie. 'The last instalment I heard was Tuba Boy Postman.'

'Well, I plucked up courage just before we went away, and I went to the sports shop to introduce myself,' says Star.

'WHAT? WITHOUT US?' screeches Lizzie.

'Well? Come on, Star, what happened?' I cry.

'He wasn't there. But I found him in the bookshop round the corner, working. He is Tuba Boy's elder brother of course. Tuba Boy's real name is Tom. And he's Saxophone Boy now!'

'AND? AND?' cries Lizzie Impatience.

'And we went to the not-very-nice café next to the shop.'

'What did you have?'

'Weak hot chocolate and a stale sponge drop with imitation cream. I have told him about the Good Looking Café, with its amaretti biscuits and lemon cakes, and he says he will make every effort to try it.'

'What did you talk about?'

She stares at me in surprise. 'Books, of course,' she says.

Of course.

Lizzie turns on me and cries, 'Now then, M! You've got news of your own. What's this double D bit you were shouting about on the way in?' She stares accusingly at my chest as if the Boob Fairy has been putting in overtime.

'Lizzie,' I say in a calm, mature, husky voice. 'I am in the sixth form now and we don't shout and shriek. It's a very long story which has nothing to do with my breast dollops. Are you sitting comfortably? Well, I'll begin by telling you that I met the Beautiful Stranger and he is very nice and gave me lots to think about.'

'AND?'

'And . . . well, I think that's the end of *The Beautiful Sightings*. Sightings of him, anyway. His eyes *are* brown but they don't make me swoon. His voice is all right but it's not the low and musical purr I dream of. It doesn't make my toes curl. I suppose it was a bit like a gorgeous actor stepping down off the silver screen after a hundred performances. Disappointing. And what finally did it for me was when he said . . .'

'What? WHAT?' they screech.

'When he said, "It's only a dog." Can you believe it? Then I saw the light. He's nice, but we have no future.'

Like I said, it's going to take a long time to catch up with all the changes in our lives.

Many an 11 o'Clock Cake will be eaten before we do.

But we've got the time and we can get the chocolate.